CHRONICLES OF THE PIED PIPER

THE RETURN TO HAMELIN

BOOK I

BY MICHAEL J. SCEPTRE

DEDICATION

This book is dedicated to Alice, my mother, who sadly passed away before seeing this book go out to the world.

I also dedicate the book to Michael and Manuel, my two best friends, cheerleaders, and sons!

TABLE OF CONTENTS

PREFACE

So long hope exists – hope for true love,
hope to find redemption, hope for peace; then,
books like this cannot be useless.

CHAPTER 1

WHERE ARE THE MISSING CHILDREN?

Somewhere in the shadows, a faint melody plays – a haunting echo of my lost flute. Or is it just the wind? The sound sends a shiver down my spine, hinting at secrets yet to be unveiled.

The stench of decay hangs heavy in the air, a pungent reminder of death's embrace. The walls, coated in a thick layer of grime, seem to absorb the dim light, creating a suffocating darkness. Dried, crimson stains mar the floor, a macabre tapestry that tells a tale of horror. I fight the urge to retch; the very thought of what these stains signify churns my stomach.

My heart pounds, a desperate rhythm in my chest, as fear and anticipation grip me. This dungeon, a hellish abyss, threatens to shatter my resolve. Memories of my past deeds haunt me—the missing children, the secrets I've kept. They weigh on me, heavy as the chains that might soon bind me. Before you know it, I'll be confessing to all sorts– the missing children, the hidden treasure, the secret animals... the lot!

With each passing second, my chances of escape dwindle. The children's faces flash before my eyes – each one a reminder of the ticking clock. If I don't act soon, their fate and mine, will be sealed.

I want to get out of here. I rack my brain. The irony of my predicament is not lost on me. The same flute, my conduit of music magic, now just a silent spectator to my fate. It's ironic, really. Once a saviour, now a mere bystander. It makes me wonder what other secrets lie dormant, like those whispered in Azwan's hallowed halls, secrets I'm yet to uncover.

Back to the matter at hand – my inevitable death, or so it seems in this macabre dance of fate. Like a grim rehearsal, this torture and looming death feel almost as if I'm practicing for an encore. Hamelin, you've not seen the last of me, I fear. First, they serve my torture as a starter, then my death as the main course – but what if this is just the opening act?

A door creaks open, the sound slicing through the silence. A silhouette looms in the doorway, moving with deliberate slowness, as if to prolong my torment. My heart races; I'm caught between dread and a defiant resolve. The silhouette moves closer, a harbinger of the immediate threat, yet my mind can't help but wander to grander schemes. This personal purgatory feels almost like a prelude, a mere shadow of the greater battle that brews beyond these stone walls. A battle of good, evil, and all the grey in between. Hamelin, Azwan, and the world beyond – what roles shall we all play in this unfolding drama?

The figure steps into the light, revealing his grotesque form. He's an old brute, his face a roadmap of scars and hardships. His one good eye fixes on me with a manic intensity. The other, lost to some unspoken horror, is covered by a filthy patch. His appearance is terrifying yet oddly fascinating.

His face is deeply scarred. Tell you what - life has been kinder to me in comparison. The gods cursed him with a protuberant beak-like aquiline pig's nose!

But who's judging?

I'm not!

I clear my throat. It was so dry that even a skunk's urine would have tasted heavenly. I am nervous. And I am also madly starving.

As the brute approaches, a locket falls from his pocket – inside, a picture of a child, one of the missing. My heart sinks.

A memory flashes before my eyes. I'm back in Azwan, the air alive with melodies only we, the students of Tiffin's School of Music, could hear. I recall my final day, standing proud yet anxious, as Master Eolin tasked me with my first mission, "Hamelin!" he had said, his voice a mix of gravity and encouragement, "a small town, but your music will work its magic! Little did I know, my music would bring about a tragedy as profound as the one I was meant to prevent!

The missing right leg I had assumed is, in fact, a wooden peg leg, concealed beneath tattered shorts. This unexpected revelation does little to comfort me as he delivers a powerful kick to my stomach.

I collapse to the cold, wet floor, pain radiating through my body.

Lying on the cold, hard floor, I can't help but think back to that fateful day in Hamelin. How young and eager I was, armed with nothing but my flute and the teachings of Tiffin. The streets of Hamelin were supposed to be my proving ground, my first step into a world that needed my music magic. But their betrayal twisted my purpose, turned an innocent ambition into a nightmare. I was supposed to be their saviour, but alas, I became their doom!

The brute pauses, his one good eye glinting with malice. 'You think you know pain, Mr Piper?' he hisses, his voice a cold whisper. 'I've barely begun.' His unpredictability is more terrifying than his blows. This isn't just about survival; it's a battle for redemption!"

He kicks me again. And again.

"You, with your tunes and tricks, thought you could play God in Hamelin. Look at you now, powerless and pitiful. We'll have justice for what you've done."

I'm no Adam, but I'd willingly give up my ribs for some relief right now. He steps back, perhaps to give his wooden peg leg a rest. He brings out a pouch from his pocket and dangles it in front of my face mockingly. Perhaps he's trying to test me. They think I love money too much. But then again, I took their children away when I didn't get paid!

The guilt still weighs heavily on me. I start to pant. I feel drowsy. He then tosses the bag of coins to my bruised face.

He stands over me, a pouch of coins in his hand. "Pay the Pied Piper," he taunts, tossing the bag onto my bruised body. "Now, where are the children, Mr. Pied Piper?" I paid a price too, you know. A price of conscience and regret. But you wouldn't understand that, would you? I snap back.

"Go on, use your Pipe," he gleefully encourages me. Oh, what a splendid idea! And perhaps the brute would like a dance to accompany the melody too.

"Charm them back, now that you have your money."

Desperation claws at me. If only I had my flute. But without it, I am helpless, unable to unleash the vengeance I yearn for upon this forsaken place. I would have brought a thousand plagues to this god-forsaken hellhole. These people still don't deserve their children.

He readies himself for another attack, and I steel myself for the inevitable pain. The room fills with the sounds of anticipation—footsteps, whispered commands, the rattle of chains. My mind races, but my body is frozen, waiting for the first strike that will mark the beginning of my torment.

"Did you hear that?

Can you hear the tip tap sounds of children running back?"

More men suddenly appear from nowhere, as if I'm in a dream. I take it the town does not allow womenfolk to see a man suffer. It might encourage some revolutionary ideas!

"Is that the sound of children I hear? You - go check outside."

"Nothing, sire. Just our children and their parents anxiously waiting to see him killed."

"I thought so. We pay the Pied Piper, and still we wonder, where are the children?"

"You are nothing but a child-thief!" he says in disgust.

I'm sure he would have loved to choke me with his hook of a hand.

As they hurl accusations, calling me all sorts of names under the sun, my mind drifts to the days before this madness. In Azwan, my music was a source of joy, a force for good. "Use your talents wisely," Master Eolin had cautioned, his eyes reflecting the sacred responsibility of our art. But in Hamelin, my talents were scorned, my purpose corrupted. It was not just the children I took that day; it was my own innocence that I lost.

"Here, your pipe - let's see if you can play a song and call your rescuers?" he says with a devilish smirk. He is enjoying this. If only they knew - they wouldn't be accusing me of being the greedy Pied Piper.

"Now, for the premier event," as he motions for men holding canes to come near me. The room is full of excitement alright. There is a lot of rumbling and evil laughter.

"Quiet between you all!" the man snarls at them. "We need to keep count of the lashes."

"Grab the other cane, the one with the thorns," he directs one of the men.

The man hurriedly obeys.

Bruce almighty! Today I'm in for a good beating.

"Ah yes. This cane will write a beautiful bloody poem across your back. Let all those who read it know what happens to those who steal children."

The men stretch their knuckles and arms in unison. My twin torturers! They've looked forward to this moment all their lives. Today, one hundred and thirty was my lucky number. That was the number of the children I'd taken away. How I wish I'd just left them all behind. I tense my body and ready myself for the beating. It can't be worse than the peg leg. That was until the first hit.

"Ein!" shouted one man.

His job was to keep count. This depends on my being able to take any more lashes though. I very much doubt he will be counting for long.

"Zwei!"

"Drei!"

"Vier!"

I am seriously doubting if I will even survive long enough to savour the rest of these lashes.

"Funf!"

"Sechs!"

"Sieben!"

"Acht!"

"Hit him harder!" shouts the old man. He is getting more animated as time goes by. I empathize with the brute; he wants to see more because he is only seeing half the action poor soul!

"WHERE ARE THE CHILDREN?" he demands.

Bound and beaten, I let my mind escape to a time of hope, to the halls of Tiffin, where every note played was a step towards a brighter future. We were young, naive perhaps, believing our music could change the world for the better. Hamelin was supposed to be the beginning, a town lifted from despair by the magic of my flute. Instead, it became the end – of my dreams, of my innocence, of a life I once knew.

Each subsequent strike is a searing line of fire across my back. I doubt my ability to endure this brutal punishment. The room spins, the chorus of counting and jeers blending into a cacophony of pain and despair.

As consciousness slips away, one thought remains: the children. Where are they? What has become of them? The darkness closes in, and I am left with only my guilt and the echoing question of my fate.

***

Oh, some light. I see some light! Is this the light at the end of the tunnel that everyone always talks about? I'm just wishing to wake up from this awful dream but alas, the agony attests that it is happening in flesh and blood.

"See him now - he can't even take the pain! Yet, he was more than happy to take our children away from us. Did you think of the untold pain you caused the parents?" he asks me.

"Sire, if we continue to whip him, he will soon die, and folks won't have a chance to see his small head being cut off."

"Ok, take him away," the old man reluctantly agrees.

The old man comes closer to inspect me with his one eye. It's much bigger than I thought. Probably overcompensating for the runaway eye.

"Why don't you do the right thing, at least tell us where the children are and die with some honour?"

I do not see my dying at the hands of such brutes being an honourable thing - my death honours them but shames my soul.

"I don't - know where they are." I reply as I wince in pain. It's difficult to speak when heavy chains are mercilessly clutching me in a choke hold while my adrenaline recedes, leaving me to bear the full brunt of the pain I've so bravely pretended to tolerate. Randomly, out of nowhere, a man spits in my face. Considering that I was going to die anyway, the saliva was a welcome antiseptic.

How did I even get here?

Unless Guernsey was nothing but a figment of a fairy tale I'd conjured up earlier. I'm still confused. Anyway, it's too late to debate how I got here. I am here, and I am about to die.

"Drag him out. Everyone is waiting for him," a stern voice barks orders from above the dungeon.

It seems the entire town is waiting to see me. At that point, it's not death that I fear most. It's the thought of how I will die that cuts my heart a thousand times. If I had wings, I would fly all the way back to Guernsey!

"Your calmness considering your dire circumstances impresses me, Mr Pied Piper," says one of the men as he ushers me out of the dungeon.

I just look at him with a pitiful eye. Any agitation will just waste away the little ounces of energy left within my feeble body. Besides, did they expect me to be in a jovial mood? Or quarrelsome? Wailing like a child without its mother, or a mother without her child, should I remorsefully say? But they taught me to never cry over spilt milk - or blood as it was in my case!

I look one more time behind me at the dark dungeon. Am I looking forward to my death, or am I missing being curled up on the icy floor? As I come out, I smell the fresh morning dew. A welcome respite for my nostrils. My lungs have suffered from the merciless stink of the place. Is it any wonder why rats found this place their utopia?

The fresh dew breathed a new lease of life into my feeble and bloodied body. I did not care if I was under-dressed for the chilly morning. Mind you, death has an interesting way of changing your perspective on what matters in life.

Everyone is keen to feast their eyes on me. I wish I could say that it's because I look exceptionally handsome, but I'm too sensible to believe that. It's as if they can't believe the reports that they have caught the infamous Pied Piper. Finally, justice has come.

Even the little children are gazing at me. Have their parents not told them about me? You would think they'd hide their children from me, wouldn't you? Blimey, I think to myself. I hope they aren't staying for the main event! Imagine these little poor innocent souls having to see my head plump into a basket!

I hope my executioner lifts my head up after chopping it off - so I can give them a quick cheeky wink for a friendly laugh before I'm done. I've never been a fan of these types of beheadings, but what does that matter anymore? Nobody will care about my opinions on capital punishment by the time my head's gone!

The men walking ahead of me seem to be really enjoying their moment in the spotlight. And I can only imagine the glory that awaits my executioner.

"Make way, make way, for the Pied Piper of Hamelin!" Yells the giant of a man in front me. Why hadn't I noticed this towering Philistine before? He is nine feet tall and gangly. Surely, he must be the ugly cousin of the one-eyed brute. And, more than happy to be towering above the crowd.

The crowd desperately wants to catch a glimpse of me for the last time. The giant is impatient. I don't blame him. That gargantuan frame must be an unwelcome heavy burden for his bones. He probably killed his mother during childbirth!

He's weary, and angrily shoves his way through the bloodthirsty crowd. Young and old, frail and strong, were all pushed aside with ease. It's as if the giant is clearing the path of dead autumn leaves. I trail behind him in chains. I feel like an ox being led to its slaughter.

"Hängen sie den kinderdieb!" shouts the hysterical crowd.

I don't speak one word of German, but my drooping face suggests otherwise. They could speak Latin for all I care. I just know I am in trouble. Big trouble!

I'm welcomed by the sound of men and women yelling, chanting, shouting, and hissing at me. Even young children join in, encouraged by their resentful parents. Some hurl stones my way while others practice the sport of spitting at me. Tell you what, warm saliva isn't entirely unwelcome as I shiver against the bitter cold. Everyone can have a go at me today, it seems. Fame has a nasty price now, doesn't it?

Despite the snow blanketing the ground, the spectacle of preparing for my execution seems to have ignited a thousand hot fire devils in the crowd's eyes - with my blood, the only thing to douse them. Only an important man could draw such a crowd. A bit of positivity for the morning before I take on the day!

But I know I am lying to myself. I am just a wandering fellow trying to make bitter juice out of life's rotten fruits. You know what? Perhaps, I deserve to die. The guillotine will mete out fair justice.

The incessant yelling and chanting grow louder as they drag me towards the graveyard. Ah, at last, the place where I will meet my brutal end is near!

My death seems an important occasion. It would purchase a thousand goodwills for the town's Mayor for sure. A better bargain than when he cheated me of my gold coins! To the Mayor, I'm the gift that keeps on giving.

The gangly man happily hands me over to my executioner. I lie. He shoves me to the ground. I can feel the gritty ooze of dirt and blood tickling my face as it drips down. I try to pull a crooked smile just to enhance the spectacle. After all, a smile makes the hard moments in life easier. I rattle my chains, trying my luck to break free myself. Perhaps, a last-minute glorious escape is on the cards.

The giant Philistine looks down at me with pity. Even if I were to free myself, the bloodthirsty crowd would dish out a worse punishment than the guillotine. Regardless, I'm too resolute to give up. I dig my feet into the mud and almost pull down my giant captor!

Like a parent babying their spoilt brat of a child, my executioner bends down and gently helps me to my feet while ignoring my poor attempts to resist.

His hands are rough. Defeated by his firm grip, I feel my body droop before I fall into the mud again. The crowd cheers even louder. They are so excited that it weirdly rubs off onto me. In return, I give a faint smile.

I notice the veins and marks on my executioner's hands. They tell a hundred tales about his bloody career! This is just another day at the office!

Standing there all alone, I become an empty soul. I have lost all hope. The mocking and spitting have finally nibbled away the last remains of my dignity.

They strip me naked. There I am, a fine specimen of a chiselled dark-skinned body for Hamelin's women to admire. Fearfully and wonderfully made. Azwan's finest! Grown men cast lots to decide who gets my clothes. Mind you, my feathered hat makes for a good souvenir.

A sweet old lady slowly approaches me. In her hand is a basket. Aww, I'm thinking she wants to feed me something before I die. My first and last meal of the day. She goes past me to place it at one end of the guillotine not so far from where I am standing. Hold on a minute, the basket is for my head it seems! Doesn't this old witch of a woman know that sooner than later she will be joining me too? I'll gladly leave the gates of hell open for her!

I gaze at the guillotine, finally paying attention to the thing that will end my life. What a deathly machine it is! Earthlings - I mean, people and their love for gruesome deaths, eh? What could go wrong?

All it needs is one mighty blow. All my executioner must do, is to use all his strength to strike me with the blade and he will earn his keep.

The executioner puts on a black mask. Wow - talk about being superstitious much! It beggars' belief! What has he got to hide from? Even if I become a ghost, I would still fear him and I'm never going to come anywhere near him!

He places my head nicely between the wooden planks. This is it!

"You better pray that I do this in one strike," he whispers in my ear. Talk about invading one's personal space! His lips are so close to my ears, I know he had a nibble of my ears wax.

"I can think of a thousand better prayers," I assure him. "But I'll reluctantly grant you your last-minute prayer request, good sir!" Even in my last moments, I'm determined to keep my sense of humour.

He slowly guides the heavy blade to the nape of my neck. He is measuring alright. I bet all my invisible gold coins that he will strike me clean. The blade feels cold on my skin, so much so, it sends shivers down my spine. It also feels awfully blunt!

"Oh, this will be fun!" I chuckle to myself. He hears me. Confusion spreads across his wrinkled face. He raises his arms, readying himself. The stakes are higher. His reputation is on the line. He owes the crowd a splendid show. One colossal blow would go a long way to secure future business. A job well done is the best outcome for the both of us.

Everyone jostles to be in the front. An adolescent boy slowly makes his way towards the platform. He is Hamelin's scribe. Too many ink markings on his clothes to suggest otherwise. First the old witch, now this little rascal of a boy!

He carries a sign with the words - THE PIED PIPER OF HAMELIN, THE CHILD-THIEF. I thought I would have a nicer eulogy than that! Don't they always say pleasant things about dead people?

I've rescued the town from rats. I've saved many kingdoms and towns from terrible things, and all they remember me for is being a child-thief?

"Any last words, Mr Pied Piper?" Asks the little rascal without a single ounce of pity in his eyes. I look at him. Does he have any idea what he is asking for? Will he even comprehend my last words? The more they make these little ones do the worst jobs in the town, the more I feel justified, again, in taking them away. But that thought better not make it out of my head with this bloodthirsty mob roundabout!

"All I have ever wanted was to love and to be loved," I declare. It sounded nobler in my head than when it came out as a child's vomit.

Next thing I know, the executioner raises both his arms about to strike.

**

Time stands still. Is this real? Even if he misses, the blow to my head will still send me on my merry way to the grave. In a moment, my head will no longer be mine. If this is a nightmare, then this is the most appropriate time to wake up. But nigh. I am still here, and everything is real and happening in slow motion.

Something flashes before me. The blade's just gone through me! Oh, my lord! Have I just witnessed my own death? I try to scream on top of my now-detached lungs. It's more of a gurgle, spitting out the last of the blood in my throat. I want to breathe. But I'm missing my body. I catch a glimpse of my torso dancing about on the platform above.

Well! I don't know what impressed me the most - the clean-cut signifying a job well done, or the fact that I experienced first-hand what it's like to have my head cut off. My eyes become heavy. I feel a sudden urge to sleep. This is surely not a dream!

Faces peer down at me in the old witches' basket. I wonder how they feel looking at my decapitated head. I try to smile again, just for old time's sake, but this time it's impossible. I am dying all right. I know I don't have long to live, but I still think it's possible that my torso could survive without my head. If Mike the Chicken could live for over a year without his head, perhaps it's time I rewrite the history books.

A person holds a rat above the basket. Oh, that's just savage! Chucking a rat into the basket to eat me up? Why can't they at least start with my chiselled body? I see the sharp, pointy teeth of the creature that looks at me with something akin to hunger in its dark, shiny eyes.

It drops into the basket, and I feel its clawed feet scurrying over my cheek. I try to shake it off, but my head won't move. It will eat me alive. The rat quickly gets to work as it nibbles my black hair.

As darkness edges my vision, a sudden revelation strikes me – a crucial memory, a missing piece. I strain against the encroaching blackness, desperate to hold onto this sliver of hope.

CHAPTER 2

THE MARBLE MACHINE

I feel something lick my ear. Is it the executioner
having a taste of me now, too? I feel the sensation
again. But this time I notice that it's rather soft,
almost affectionate-like. Why would my
executioner be affectionate to me? It makes no
sense. Something about this situation bothers me
deeply. If I'm dead, how can I feel anything at all?
How do I feel aware of my body when I have had
my head severed? Somehow, I don't think my
powers can prepare me for a bizarre, out-of-body
sensation and, even if I had the powers to do it, it'd
be difficult to make it appear as normal as it does
now.

A droplet falls on my face; it feels gooey, and
I look around again. It's Fatso! My pet rat, laying
over a bed while looking at me with a playful gleam
in his eyes. I look around once again and notice that
I'm lying on a soft surface. Then it hits me. I'm on
my bed, safe, after running away from Hamelin.
And then the shock washes over me and gives place
to something else. Relief flows through me, and I
thank the universe for this was only an awful dream.
I glance around the room and blink as I'm
momentarily blinded by the sunlight entering
through the window.

Oh-my-goodness! I'm still alive! Well, hold on. Am I alive like Mike the Chicken or alive-alive? What's this? These wild strands of dishevelled locks. I must be having a foul hair day again! I quickly comb my fingers down my locks a few times to fix it.

Oh, what's this? It seems to be my neck all right. And...it's still attached to my body! I've never been this grateful to wake up in one piece in my entire life. I grab at my neck frantically once again and pinch my arm just to check that I'm really here, alive, and I conclude that I am okay.

"You scared me, buddy," I tell Fatso. I was both annoyed and happy at his antics. He doesn't answer like the others do, he's not capable of speaking; licking my face is his way of communicating with me.

Fatso emits a small sound. He goes straight to my arm and gives it an affectionate lick. He gives me a look of worry too. I make a mental note to be better, my distress must have terrified him poor thing. Fatso easily gets stressed, and I wouldn't want him to be any more nervous than he normally is. If I want this to be worth it, I need to assure my friends they'll be safe in our new home. Although, I doubt I have the skills to keep him and the others safe.

I'm okay though, I only had an awful dream. I'm glad Fatso is here with me, although I'm not a fan of having my hair licked this early or ever. It usually leaves my dreadlocks looking like a mess for hours. I don't think I could chastise him though, even if he does truly anger me. He's too innocent and loyal to a fault.

I do wonder if I should have brought them all here. I don't know if they are safe here. All I can do is play my music and hope for the best.

I gaze out the lofty window right across from my four-poster bed, delighted to find the bright dawn illuminating the garden outside of my vast house. Not to brag, but this house is only fit for an Azwan rebel. Someone in exile, like myself. With purple orchids, tangerine tiger lilies, and sun yellow tulips all in bloom, one would soon forget their home. Next to the flowers is a towering, lush thicket. Beyond this scenic backyard, the turquoise sea lazes languidly at the foot of the immense mountains in the distance.

I crack open the window and take one gulp of fresh morning air, relieved to find myself safe in my beloved Guernsey. I've never seen it this green before! There are patches of small flowers with so many colours; there's yellow, violet, and red flowers of all shapes. I can't pick a favourite. I like all the vibrant colours. Far ahead, I can see a vast land made of tall, robust trees with abundant foliage.

My consciousness is awakening slowly to the beauty of the island. Tracing paths through the hazy state of my brain, I keep recounting the things I like about this place. I'd take insomnia any day over going to sleep again!

A soft knock sounds on the front door. I am spooked by it. Even though I live alongside all kinds of animals, after that horrid dream, I can't help but expect the worst.

I fasten my brocade dressing gown over my linen pyjamas. As I approach the hallway, I notice a few teacups in need of washing still scattered along my desk. They were next to a chaotic stack of music sheets I'd composed, specially tailored to the finicky ears of various pests I'd one day lure away and rescue Earthlings once more. I'm about to reach for my flute but retreat my hand when a shiver runs down my spine. I can't dare to play the very music that made me Hamelin's arch-enemy and prompted this all-too-realistic nightmare of mine!

I slowly open the door and, lo-and-behold, it's my pet deer! Behind her, prancing in, are the glorious unicorn horses, as sprightly as an animal could be this early in the morning. Bolt and Storm, my trusted unicorns and the most rebellious of the group, dash into the room without even acknowledging my presence, hopping, and sliding across the parquet floor. Bolt collides right into my desk and sends the music sheets flying across the floor and two teacups shattering to shards next to it.

To my surprise, Fatso scurries out of one of the broken cups, holding a piece of carrot between his tiny paws. He squeaks a hello to the group as if I am invisible. "Are you ok, Fatso?" I ask, picking him up and putting him back to safety on the table.

"First you chew my hair to wake me up, now this!" I heave a sigh.

"Morning, morning! - why do you look so nervous?" Coco asks as she leads her fawns, Enya, and Cookie into the house.

"Well, besides Bolt and Storm causing havoc again," I begin, clearing my throat, "I had another nightmare."

"Again?" She asks in disbelief. "You should get help for that!"

"Aha," I say dubiously. "And where can I find the nearest shrink to cure me of the guilt that I feel for taking Hamelin's children away?"

"Or you could just go back to Hamelin and say you're sorry," she squeaks.

"Yes, I can imagine that would give them some closure - the power of words ey?" Storm chimes in, as his younger brother is still energetically bobbing across my floor.

"Why are you here?" I finally ask. It's rare for the deer to come inside my house unless they are having trouble with the lions again. Mind you, it's very hard to convince lions that they can survive on a plant-based diet. I must remind them again, either they live in peace or look for meat back in the actual world! But the lions keep bothering the deer anyhow, and that doesn't seem to change soon. Maybe I should sell them to a travelling circus. But my pets wouldn't survive long out in the wild and they know it.

"Is it the lions again?" I press.

As I wait for Coco to vent about those big, golden, furry beasts roaring and flashing their sharp teeth at her all morning, I feed my other pet, Boris the Spider. He was a gift from Asia, and many fear him, but he's so gentle and kind. Round and fuzzy, with four shiny black eyes, as cute as can be. He's the closest to a son I have.

"Morning!" He says in his little boy's voice. I'd always thought, if I had a wife, she would love him too.

"A-hem," Coco clears her throat to get my attention. She's always been envious of how attentive I am to Boris.

"Yes?" I reply as if already predicting her next words.

"Um, we don't know how you will take this," she begins, throwing me off guard. "But we would rather go back to the wild." She casts her doe eyes downwards.

Of all my pet deer, she's the most confident, but I can tell she had to muster up enough courage to tell me this. Storm and Bolt quickly duck behind her.

"But you won't survive for long out there by yourselves!" I protest.

"Don't let my veganism fool you into thinking Earthlings or other wild lions won't come after you."

I've never been able to eat animals. The mere thought revolts me. If animals are my friends, how can I eat them? It's inconceivable.

"It's not that - we have everything we want here, but we miss our friends and family terribly."

"That is rich considering that there's plenty of you who can keep each other company, whereas there is only one of me!"

"We just want to be with our friends," Coco reasons.

"You know, other deer who look like us, talk like us, think like us - that's all."

"Ok. Why don't I bring them over here and then you won't have to risk your lives to see them?"

"Oh, that could work," Coco quickly agrees.

"W-wait a minute," I falter. "That was too easy. You never wanted to leave, did you?" As I realise that they were bluffing and they tricked me again.

Did I forget to mention that not only is Coco a confident deer, but she is a darn smart one too? They all hurry out of the house to play in the backyard.

"Thanks a million," Coco shouts as she disappears into the woodlands.

"Would you also like new friends too, Boris?" I asked him half-jokingly as I look into his shiny watery eyes. I can tell he wants to say yes but doesn't want to offend me.

"Ok, I will see if I can find you some playmates," I say anyway.

"Thank you," Boris replies in his juvenile voice.

"This Guernsey castaway needs some good ol' breakfast!" I think out loud, trying to cheer myself up.

As I step out of the room, I hear little Boris clear his throat, as if about to tell me something. I turn around.

"Oh, it's nothing," he blurts out. He takes a few nervous paces in circles on the table.

"Do you love us or are you having to put up with us?" He finally chokes out.

The mere question saddens me. I go over to him and gently pet his fuzzy back with my fingers.

"I do love you guys – you are my only friends," I reassure him.

He pulls a smile, at least wanting to believe me. While walking over to the kitchen, I reflect on the situation. I love them all but talk about being ungrateful. They have everything they could ever want. Out here, on the island, in bliss, they never have to fear for their lives. Also, I played some music to keep them young forever. And yet, they still demand more playmates!

I then grab my bean jar which I left to slow cook overnight, all the while recounting that nightmare. My one-of-a-kind recipe is perfect. Although I have lived alone for many years, I still cook for two. It just feels odd to do otherwise. Deep down inside, I think I secretly hope that one day, I will have someone to share my life with.

Just as I wallow in my loneliness, Sherbert and Pepe, my ravens, glide through the open window.

"SKRRA PAP KA SKIDIKI PA PAP!" Sherbert sings in a mischievous tone.

Sherbert and Pepe are inseparable. They are twin ravens, which is a unique thing for ravens. I consider them my lucky charms. There's a peculiar essence to their energy when the twins are around that calls to my soul. They're also mischievous and have taken a liking to singing to me loudly, something they know bothers me. This seems to be their way of thanking me for getting them out of that place. They respect me but pranking me seems to be the best way to lighten the mood.

"Stop that!" I shout at them in annoyance.

In the past few weeks, they have ventured to the west of Africa. It is where they picked up the hideous-yet-hilarious morning greeting. What else can I expect from the haughty Ravens?

Sherbet and Pepe were gifts from the Greeks. I'd helped one of the Greek islands with their rat troubles. Besides the gold coins, they gave me Sherbert and Pepe while they were still small hatchlings. If only I knew they would grow to be this much trouble!

A Greek old Earthling had told me that the ravens in their previous lives had been loyal servants to the Greek god called Odin. He was a control freak and would often make the ravens spy for him. Something I've learnt to appreciate about having them about.

"Anything interesting today besides the Skrra pap pappitty whatever you said?"

"SKIBIDI PAP PAP PA PA SKIAAA!" Pepe continues to annoy me. He's perched up on my kitchen table while he preens his glossy black wings.

I raise my eyebrows as if to ask if they could stop.

"SKIAAA" they both shout as they fall over on the table laughing. They always seem to have fun between themselves. It's the laughs, the inside jokes, the camaraderie, the trust - they have a special bond them two.

I wish I had a best friend. Someone inseparable from me. Just to laugh at silly things. With these mischievous birds, I've already given up on trying to stop them from teasing me. It's in their nature.

I sit down and try to enjoy my bean jar, spoonful by spoonful, attempting to ignore this pair who never have a dull moment. I am jealous of them though.

"So, have you found a suitable woman during your travels, or you were busy perfecting your newfound greeting?" I tease.

Suddenly they stop laughing. They both jerk up and jump back onto the windowsill.

"What - did you not find anyone then?" I demand. Otherwise, why would they be so apprehensive?

"Well, are you going to talk?" I make eye contact with Sherbert, the more courageous of the two.

"We have found you an exquisite damsel of a girl."

"Oh!" My eyes widen in anticipation.

I move my chair closer. "Is that so? Did she pass the Pied Piper test?" I enquire.

"Oh, yes. She even shared some of her bread with us."

"It's impressive considering that she is a downright pauper," Pepe chimes in.

"How could you tell?" I ask as my curiosity grows.

"The entire place reeked of poverty," Sherbert explains with disgust.

"Humans sat outside were gnawing at leather belts and shoes for food."

My gut churns at the idea that Earthlings could be suffering because of me. I don't know how or why, but these days it seems like the Pied Piper is to blame for everything. Pepe is blissfully unaware of my internal distress. He keeps casually feeding me all the gory details of the town's suffering. It does sound eerily familiar though.

"There were so many homeless people in the streets," Pepe adds.

"Is that so?" I ask, while toying with the idea of going to rescue my damsel in distress.

"Um, I think I'll go outside for some fresh air," Pepe excuses himself, soaring off into the garden.

"What's going on with him?" I ask. "He never leaves you by yourself."

Sherbert just shrugs.

"What's the problem? Is she already married to an Earthling?"

"Oh no, it's not that at all."

"Then what?" I beseech, extending my arms in desperation for an answer.

"Promise you won't be angry with us?"

"Why would I? You've made remarkable progress on this mission, probably the most important one of my life. She's beautiful, she cares, she passed the Pied Piper test. Then what else could be wrong?"

"Then it wouldn't bother you if the special lady is from, ahem - Hamelin?" Sherbert mumbles. He squints his eyes as if expecting me to shout at him or smash something.

"Oh." I just freeze. Pepe then perches back onto the windowsill, switching his gaze between the both of us. I look down at my bean jar, but now it just seems like a murky swamp of tasteless mush.

So, let me get this straight. I've just woken up from a nightmare in Hamelin! Coco has just tricked me into another quest far away to go find her friends to play with. Boris also would like a playmate, and mind you, Asia was no close neighbour for retrieving that. Now, the happy-go-lucky ravens have brought me splendid news, but quickly pierced me with the Hamelin dagger. The best news is that my would-be-wife could end up getting me caught in Hamelin and probably play witness to my head being chopped off and used as a wedding dowry to appease her father.

"You realise that, today, I had the worst nightmare of my life," I stammer. "I suffered torture and my beheading was the icing on the cake. And now you expect me to marry one of Hamelin's own daughters? Should I be reminding you again, that it was I, the Pied Piper, who took all their children away?"

"How much do you think they would demand for her dowry?" Sherbert asks, at which Pepe explodes into a fit of laughter.

"Erm, how about one hundred and thirty Hamelin children, and your head?" I reply in a German accent, trying to mimic the would-be-in-laws.

"But, sire, you promised not to get angry," Sherbert politely reminds me.

"Oh no, I am not angry. I am just trying to imagine how it will go down for me to marry this girl."

"If all else fails, you have the flute. You can lure her away like you did with the other children," Pepe insensitively suggests.

I get up and shut the windows and leave them outside to continue their jesting without me. They just don't get it. And what do they do then? The two Ravens continue to peck at the glass.

"Skraa Pa Pa!"

I close the curtains and go upstairs to my music room, throwing myself down on the chair in front of my music stand. Nubian musical instruments of all types fill up the room. It's been a mess of late with my not getting enough sleep. I grab the Djembe as I want to get energised. But I don't feel the energy to make any magic happen in this room.

"Skraa Pa Pa!" I hear a faint shout from the music room. Then a titter. They say Ravens are some of the smartest creatures in the world, but they sure have no tact.

"Skraa Pa Pa!"

Are you kidding me? I look over to the windowsill, finding Angel, the lyrebird. He glances at me with a jolly glow in his eyes, proud of the new phrase he's learned. He playfully wiggles his bright, long tail of orange, black, and blue.

"You too?"

You do not understand how hard it is to be the one and only Pied Piper. Goodness gracious, I need to go back in time! Perhaps it is somewhere else in the world that I can make these nightmares stop. A small adventure won't be so bad if it gets me out of this grim mood. I want to go somewhere where I am not the villain for once.

I spring up from my chair and approach the marble machine. It's one of my favourite instruments. Its magical melodies can take me anywhere in time. I need to escape to somewhere with sweet memories. The brass disc sat with a gleaming marble archway standing tall above. It embeds a plethora of crystals and gems within the brass archway.

Standing in the archway, I recall a melody of recollection, the kind that makes one calm their thoughts and think about the good old times. The time machine ran on powerful emotions brought forth by the magical melodies of the flute that only I could summon.

Standing in the middle of the disc and archway, I pulled out my black flute, glossy and expertly crafted with rings of gold near the mouthpiece. With my pet rat Fatso poking his head out of my vest pocket to watch, I play the notes in a rising minor melody. The tune fills the room with a haunting tone and the gems in the machine glow beautifully. An array of resplendent blue and red colours shined from the machine, creating a tear in the archway, one that had a glowing blue light that swirled with incandescent brilliance.

"Well then, Fatso, let us be off!" I call my companion as we step into the light together. The light stretched into a rush of a tunnel, with various lights passing by us as if they were stars. Fatso and I were weightless through the streaming expanse where time ceased to exist. After a matter of seconds, the stream flattened into a stable frame, time starting to coalesce back into the normal world as a foreign landscape appeared before me.

Day turns into night. I have time travelled all right. Blurry images reach my eyes. We are back in Asia. Central Asia, to be precise. I know this because I can see my favourite Earthlings - the Mongols! I see my happy self, walking carefree in the streets.

I spot a man with a goatee in the crowd gathered about my younger self. They are all clapping and merry. He seems impressed with the Pied Piper. There was a time they appreciated me. I need to remind myself of this.

A little girl withdraws from the crowd to approach the Pied Piper. O how I miss being loved! However, I need to keep reminding myself that I have time travelled. It will soon end.

The girl hands over a box. In it is a spider. It's Boris! Still a tiny itsy bitsy spider then. A worthy gift for single-handedly stopping the black death that was sweeping across the continent wiping everything in its path!

"Domo Arigato," the girl says as she bows.

The Pied Piper bows in return. He is humbled by the many gifts he is receiving. More kids come out of nowhere with gifts in their hands. What a grateful bunch they were - I would have rid the place of a thousand plagues! I scream in a whisper.

The kids overwhelm the Pied Piper with the gifts. He jumps back onto his unicorn. As the Pied Piper slowly rides out of the town, waving incessantly back at the townsfolk, I see Pepe and Sherbet joining him.

"We just need a little wee favour," said Pepe and Sherbert at the same time. "There is a tiny wee of a town that has rat problems, and if you don't stop it, there will be a second coming of the black death across the whole continent!" warned Sherbert.

I remember this was how I ended up going to Hamelin. If only I knew it would land me in such a fiery mess afterwards.

Time fast forwards, and Hamelin is in view. I want to go back to Guernsey now. But I am curious to relive my nightmare one more time. Many rats are biting the little Earthling children. Other rats chewing and munching clothes. I spot a man running outside his house, screaming that a rat has bit his trouser snake.

A few men nearby snicker at his reaction, but it doesn't last as a rat comes forward and bites one of the men on the head. He yelps and caresses his bald head, never stopping from complaining of pain the whole time.

"Oh, I see you're not so manly, huh?" exclaims the other man holding onto to his crotch.

"At least I don't run away from rats like a baby!" snapped back the bald man.

Elsewhere, I see a woman and her children armed with pans and pots battling the rats; although the wisp of a boy looks more interested in playing with them and the woman looks downright murderous. The woman shrieks as a rat attacks her.

"You lot can be trouble sometimes," I exclaim while casting a one-eyed glance at Fatso. I wondered what he made of this.

I see the Pied Piper walk through the town square. He makes his way to the town-hall.

"I should have left this forsaken place immediately." I quietly mumble to myself.

"There's no use! I'm telling you. No one knows where they come from!" the Mayor shouts angrily.

"But if we do nothing, sire. They will kill us all!" retorts another man sat in the council.

"Woe unto Hamelin," shouts another.

"I cannot believe I helped these bunch of whoreson caterpillars!" I react angrily, as I see the Pied Piper enter the room. The Pied Piper swings the door open.

"Good evening gentlemen, it seems you have a rat problem, and I am here to offer my help," says the Pied Piper.

The men become furious. The Mayor gives the Pied Piper a withering look and several of the men attempt to seize him, but the Mayor stops them with his big round belly.

"I mean no harm," the Pied Piper reassures them.

"Who are you?" the plump Mayor asks.

"We have an enormous problem on our hands," agreed the Mayor.

"But we don't have time for your theatrics and acting. This is a very serious business which you're interrupting!", another man nervously chimes in.

"We have had it with you necromancers!" says a brown-haired man.

"We need not any more snake-oil," shouts another.

"I've just come from Asia, and I'm on my way to Baghdad. A little birdie told me you have a problem with rats. I'm here to help," the Pied Piper confirms. I cringe watching my former self wanting to help these useless Earthlings.

The Mayor excitedly shouts, "We will give you fifty-thousand gold coins if you get rid of the rats at this very moment."

The Pied Piper pauses, giving careful thought to the Mayor's proposal. "Is that a deal?" The Pied Piper asks.

"Even one hundred thousand gold coins," shouts another.

"I'll take a thousand gold coins," says the humble Pied Piper.

I should have known they would say anything just to get me to help them. The Pied Piper walks out with a confident smile on his face. The Mayor and the council rush to the balcony to watch the proceedings.

The Pied Piper plays the flute. Sweet melodies come out of his flute. The rats come out of everywhere. They follow the Pied Piper down to the Weser river. And they disappear one by one. Fatso closes his eyes firmly. This makes for a terrible horror show.

Hamelin's people come out of their houses. One by one, the adults and the children step onto the streets. Next thing, there is a joyful cheer about the place. It satisfies the Pied Piper. The proud Mayor comes to the balcony to bask in his stolen glory and adulation.

"Not to be a party popper - but my thousand gold coins," asks the Pied Piper.

"Erm—Erm," the Mayor hesitates. He quickly retreats into the town-hall. One of his council men shuts the balcony windows.

"If he thinks I will give him anything, he's a loony," the Mayor says in a booming voice.

"What are you going to do then, sir?" says the red-haired man looking conflicted.

"He'll go away, he seems a reasonable man. Surely he'd know I would not pay such an outrageous sum of money."

"But he helped us in our time of need!" the man reminds the Mayor.

The Pied Piper bursts into the town-hall. "I need my thousand gold coins now!" demands the Pied Piper.

"Or else what? You threaten us, fellow? Do your worst," the Mayor taunts him.

"Blow your pipe till you burst!" The Mayor mocks him while carrying a wide evil smug.

I remember getting hot headed. I just thought to myself, what is the best revenge on such a small little place.

The Pied Piper angrily leaves the town-hall. The Mayor and his friends rush to the balcony again. They slowly open the doors to take a peek of the Pied Piper leaving the town.

"Sire, if you leave without taking payment, worse punishment awaits them!" warns Pepe.

"They deserve it. I want none of it - let the music elves come deal with them!" the Pied Piper replies angrily.

"It won't end well," Sherbet exclaims.

The Pied Piper turns around and goes back to Hamelin. It's painful to watch this moment. The Pied Piper plays the flute one more time. This time, the Mayor and his council are dumbstruck. Even the adults of the town are also dumbstruck too. But the children - they are merry. They dance along the streets as they follow the Pied Piper. The Pied Piper heads for the hills, and a portal opens up where one-by-one the children disappear except for the one who is lame.

The Pied Piper is willing the boy to make it, but he is too far behind, and the portal is about to close. As soon as the Pied Piper jumps in, me and Fatso find ourselves back in the music room.

CHAPTER 3

TROUBLE IN HAMELIN

Flakes of snow swept through the December air, blanketing Hamelin's main square. A thick layer of white collected atop the roof of the Town Hall. The facade of the building had three ornate steeples, and four rows of windows framing an immense door. At the top of the centre steeple was a golden clock, which struck two p.m., the hour that Bob, the Mayor, had called a meeting to discuss the dire times that Hamelin was suffering.

The Mayor was an uncaring man that did as he pleased and loved to collect taxes under the guise of caring about the townspeople's wellbeing. He was going through a rough time now, dealing with the aftermath of not having enough food to feed the hungry people. People were so angry and tired, that they were willing to attempt murder and he was worried that he'd be soon murdered at the hands of an angry mob.

"I WANT FOOD!" someone shouted.

"I NEED TO FEED MY PETS!" screamed a clear female voice.

"HE HAS OUR FOOD AND MONEY!" shouted a third person.

Lastly, a fourth person shouted, "HE'S RIGHT THERE! LET'S TAKE HIS MONEY AND FOOD!"

Things quickly went downhill. He peered at the townspeople with a look of almighty rightfulness.

"Ungrateful little beasts," he muttered to himself. He always thought the world would be a better place if he could dispose of the rotten apples first. Starting with the ones that had screamed and ending with those that were poor and so lazy that they didn't even have the courage to voice their opinions.

They should know better than to anger him this way. They were lower than the ground he was touching with his shiny, new shoes. He was the picture of a smart, understanding ruler as he was. Under a past regime, they'd been hung already, and there he was, granting them the luxury of existing.

He took pride in his commanding presence and made use of it. He only needed a little help from Lez to turn everything around for him. After all, Lez was, for all intents and purposes, his pawn, his secret weapon to keep Hamelin's anger at bay.

A small drop of sweat travelled down his forehead, and he produced a handkerchief from his breast pocket and proceeded to wipe his face. An important businessman, erm, ruler like him could only look the best he could in public!

He cleared his throat and, with his head held high, ignored the growing sentiment of hatred directed at him. It would soon come to pass; of that, he was sure. These fools always felt the need to complain about things they could easily solve on their own.

Now, the Piper being blamed was a rightful position for the townspeople, but he didn't like the idea of having all this hatred directed at him too. Perspiration clung to his fine clothes as he looked around him, expecting inspiration to give him a way out of this mess.

"Order, order!" shouted the Mayor, as he stood in front of the crowd. He was a round man with a crooked smirk, and tufts of wispy black hair framing his shiny bald head. The voices of the old men surrounding him faded to hushes in preparation for the council meeting. The scribe, a young man of not more than eighteen, dipped his feather pen in a well of ink, preparing to record the minutes on his parchment.

"Do we have anything else to discuss today or are we going to keep bleating on about our woes again?" the Mayor began in a harsh tone. "I know things are bad, the fisherman drawing in empty nets each day, and some have resorted to eating worms, some even worse, eating leather belts and sandals and what not!"

"It's a sad affair that you'd rely so much on meat and fish in the first place, ask yourselves, why you're so dependent on this" he said coolly. "I don't think I should explain to you that lentils and vegetables in general have a greater nutritional value than animal beasts do! Have you lot considered the Mediterranean diet?" he asked evenly.

The crowd at the townhall booed, and a small stone was thrown at him. He glanced around, terrified of the people in front of him, wishing he could swat them away, like the annoying flies they were. Then he saw a small face peer at him from the crowd; the sad face belonged to a tear-stained boy who was alone in the crowd. He looked feral, with his brown eyes wide-open, and his nose and cheeks covered in grime.

Something about him made the Mayor pause. It wasn't pity that he felt, but hope. He knew in his heart that if he treated the poor better, people would start speaking about how nice he was. It was a win-win situation: they would stop talking nonsense, and he'd be able to focus on his flawless political career. Perhaps he could feed him and give his mother a small amount of coin to make up for their troubles. The Mayor could arrange for the boy to get a much-needed bath, some new clothes, and that would make him look like the wise, compassionate leader he thought himself to be.

He would do this if he could tolerate people at all. The mere thought of having to touch a dirty hand, or an arm, if he were to ever visit a home for his political campaign - put a stop to his half-formed plans. He couldn't bear the thought of such pitiful company. The mere thought made bile rise in his throat, and he found it difficult to say anything at all. They were dirty scum that hadn't learnt how to fend for themselves and relied on the government for help. He was a generous ruler, but even this was too much for him.

"I can assure you that there's nothing wrong being a lover of plants and herbs like me. It'll make you healthy and prosper. Besides, meat is too expensive to produce! We barely have enough production for a couple of weeks, and it won't be enough for all homes. I'm exhorting you, at this moment, to cooperate and reduce your food rations, and make use of what this beautiful land gives us freely. You won't regret it; it has worked wonders for me," he spoke sweetly to his audience and moved his fat arm to point at his round grotesque shape.

In the audience, someone started to laugh bitterly, and mocking him, and spoke: "Of course, he wouldn't eat a cow! He's a cow himself!" exclaimed a bony, short man on the row near where Bob, the Mayor was standing.

A guard gave him a menacing look and the men stepped back. Even if they were right, they knew there was no way they were winning this argument. The crowd jeered excitedly, and he felt the heavy stares of the starved, frenzied people he so fervently despised. Well, not all of them, but the poor ones he did hate and there was an abundance of them in this population.

"He's eaten all the fish!" exclaimed a fragile, pale woman. "Can't you see that he's the one eating all our food?"

"Yes! What gives him the right to do so?" demanded another one with bright red hair that came up to her chin. Her cheeks were so hollowed that she looked ready to faint in the spot, but her eyes were bright with hatred. A small baby was in her arms, quiet and observing.

The Mayor felt a shudder run up his back. Why would someone poor chose to have more children? She was sharing her misery with a small child and placing the blame on him.

"I haven't eaten any fish," he said. He found fish disgusting, all he liked to eat was red meat and sweet fruit; he was partial to all types of food that wasn't too dry, or too simple in taste.

"How can you accuse me of this when it's clearly a trick on that evil man's repertoire? He's known to kill innocent children, I would not put it past him to lure the fish out of the lake too!"

"But how could the fish follow him?" asked the woman defiantly.

"I don't know. He's the cursed magician, I'm just here trying to save us all from imminent death at the hands of his magical games. We're all his pawns here. Don't be deluded into thinking that I'm anything other than a victim too!" he said. "And I would really appreciate it, ma'am, if you kept yourself from speaking to me in such a disrespectful tone of voice. It sets a bad example for the little child."

He exhaled slowly. Besides, the weak wouldn't survive these trying times anyway, leaving him only having to focus on the people that were worth his time - the rich folks of Hamelin.

"It'd do you well to remember that no one cared about this town until I came into power!" he bellowed loudly, in a tone that left no room for further discussion.

"Who gave you the rights to speak freely? Before me, no one allowed the less privileged to speak! I'm the only one who's bothered to care about you all," he said. "And now, I'm asking you to join me in the task of taking down this man that has hurt us all so much. He's disgraced us and our children and, if he ever knew you're rising against me, he'd be so happy!" he exclaimed.

"And, oh, you wish for him to take my position as well!"

"He's an evil man and so are you!" exclaimed the little boy defiantly.

"You child, have no idea what you're talking about. I've given everything I have to this town!" exclaimed Bob. How dare such a filthy boy speak to him this way. He should cast his eyes low, and speak in a low, obedient tone of voice in front of him!

He had a disdain for poor people. He'd always believed that poor people had no one else to blame but themselves.

"But sir, if the town cannot eat or feed their families, then what other business can we talk about?" one of the council members interjected.

"When we go back to the streets what are we going to tell the rest of the people?" another man agreed. "Surely we cannot keep blaming the Pied -"

"SILENCE! You Piper," the Mayor shouted back to the rebellious council member. Any person who sympathized with the Pied Piper was called a Piper, and that title came with an unwanted burden in Hamelin. "Do any of you take sides with this PIPER here?" the Mayor demanded angrily.

A few of the men lowered their gaze. "If the Pied Piper can lure the rats away, if he can take our children away - do you think he cannot lure our fish away? We have no one else to blame but ourselves gentleman. We sympathized with that wandering fellow before, and if it wasn't for me, he would have robbed us of everything!"

"The fisherman will have to go fish in other towns if they're going to feed Hamelin," one of the council members agreed.

The Mayor cleared his throat proudly, "We cannot do all the thinking for them gentleman." And those were his final words as he made his way past the crowd as if they were invisible throughout the meeting.

Lez walked slowly, struggling to meet the steps of the podium, where the Mayor had been addressing the rumours and questions of his angry audience. Lez marvelled at how proud the man seemed when speaking. He didn't seem to be as phased by their threats as he ought to be If Lez was the one facing a multitude of angry townspeople, he'd be telling the truth. But there he was, the Mayor busy concocting lies and half-truths that angered them even more.

His work, as the town's only journalist, was getting to know what was important to the Mayor, and, through his column in the local newspaper, stir up the minds of the people against the Pied Piper while putting the Mayor in favourable light. It always worked a treat!

"There you are - my favourite Mayor!" Lez greeted him, finding Mayor Bob in front of the Town Hall. The Mayor often struggled to come down the steps, heaving to catch his breath. He was sweating bucket loads despite the nippy cold temperature outside.

The Mayor, panting from his descent, paused to bask in the adulation he expected but did not receive. "Ah, the burdens of leadership," he sighed theatrically, "If only those poisonous bunch-backed toads could feel the same!" His eyes scanned the crowd, seeking admiration, yet finding none.

The Mayor nearly lost his balance when a group of children sped past him, laughing, and screaming as they chased a ball down the street. The two had to dodge a few carts full of fruits and vegetables on their way through the town square. Hamelin buzzed with liveliness - merchants bartering, horses neighing, and infants crying in their mothers' arms. A herb vendor extended a bouquet of thyme to the two men, hoping against hope to get just a single gold coin from the stingy couple. The Mayor merely grimaced, without a hint of empathy. Instead, to the vendor's surprise, Lez dug into his pocket and gave her a handful of coins, and her eyes lit up with joy.

"I just wanted to run something by you -" Lez began.

"I also wanted to ask you a favour," interrupted the Mayor as he fumbled for his favoured handkerchief to pat away beads of sweat. He proceeded to snort into the wet cloth and proceeded to wipe his face with it too. Lez pursed his lips, his eyes darting away from the disgusting sight.

"Yes, I wanted to ask you to write a piece about how the Pied Piper stole our fish away," he continued as he folded his handkerchief and put it away.

"And this time, I'll allot you a special Christmas bonus: a crate full of fresh fish straight from Steinhude. I've made quite a handsome profit from the tulips this year and your work won't go unrewarded I can assure you."

Lez paused for a moment, trying to digest the Mayor's request.

"Yes, yes," he finally agreed. He had no other choice, given that the Mayor was the sole patron of his newspaper, the Daily Enquirer.

"I am still thinking of the perfect headline Sire."

"Whatever you do, blame all our troubles on the Piper!" was the Mayor's only request.

"Yes, of course." After a moment, Lez's lips stretched into a wry smile. "How about - THE PIED PIPER Who STOLE HAMELIN'S CHRISTMAS?" His eyes glistened with excitement.

"Ah! What a genius you are! No wonder you have my utmost trust."

All it took was one statement of praise for Lez to forgive and see past the Mayor's disgusting snorty habits.

"Now see to it that you write it, and whatever else you want to write," the Mayor assured, as he headed towards the street market.

Lez had to follow him from behind. It was slightly difficult for him to keep up with the Mayor, because although the Mayor walked rather slow, Lez kept limping through their hurried walk. Lez had to rely on a cane if he wanted to walk faster, but he wasn't carrying one with him at that moment.

"Keep up! I don't have all day to be here, I have a matter of utmost importance to attend to and a very short time to see to it!" said the Mayor.

Lez took a deep breath and ignored the unpleasant feeling the conversation was giving him.

"Sire, I thought to write some ideas of what else the townspeople could be doing, now that the river Weser has been cursed by the Pied Piper!"

"Farming my boy! Anything that doesn't move or breathe, the Pied Piper cannot lure away - so potatoes, carrots - the LOT!"

"You are far too wise Sire - What would Hamelin do without you?" Lez praised the Mayor. Although he didn't feel any admiration for the man. It was best to look the part of the blind follower, if he ever wanted to achieve his secret quest.

"I know - I know," the Mayor doubly agreed.

***

A fisherman trudged through the snow, his thick boots crunching it with each footstep. The Weser River was still on that calm winter afternoon, reflecting the silvery blue sky.

He strolled wearily towards his waterside home and pulled open the door of his house, attempting to mask the emptiness of his basket. The only thing he brought with himself were copies of the Daily Enquirer detailing the crimes of the infamous Pied Piper. He wished he could give that devil of a man a taste of his own medicine. See if he liked it when the police caught him and gave him nothing but stale bread and water.

"Why back so early, the sun has not set yet?" his wife asked, looking up from the kitchen table where she was peeling potatoes. "Did you catch anything today?" She asked with a hopeful tone.

"They are all gone! There is not a single fish to be found in the river. Never in my life have I seen such a thing!" the man replied in despair, placing his fishing rod in the cupboard. Beside it hung a giant net and a lantern above a spare pair of boots for when the other pair became soaked. He could already hear his stomach growling loudly.

"Surely, the town of Hamelin has been cursed. We should have paid that young you-know-who his money. First, he took our children away, and now, the fish as well! Is there no end to this evilness?" his wife bemoaned.

"Pay the Pied Piper will forever be a tragic lesson for us all."

"Hold your tongue woman!" the fisherman barked. "You know that we do not speak his name in this town!" He sank into a wooden chair with a frustrated thump. "Unless you are a PIPER of course!" he added. "Oh, Piper this, Piper that - you are always banging on about that fellow as if it will solve anything!" he continued to chastise her.

His wife flashed him a bitter look, trying to stifle her anger. She threw down the potato she'd peeled and seized the next one.

"I will have the Gustavo come and arrest you this very moment," he continued. "You speak of the Piper as if you wish he had also taken you away!"

His wife jumped up from the chair. She lanced the potato peels in the trash with one violent slam. "Who cares if I mention his name – our so-called Mayor, huh? The fat dwarf of a man who declared the souls of our children to be less valuable than a purse of guilders! Damn him, and damn anyone who follows his ridiculous rule," she spat. "The town of Hamelin cast the first stone, and now we live with the consequences."

"Listen to yourself!" the fisherman retorted. "The Piper could have done things differently. If anybody deserves eternal damnation, it is him and his greedy lust for vengeance. If he ever dares show his face in this town again, I shall take that Pipe of his and wedge it sideways up his backside"

"You only need to give a look to the newspaper stories that have been published! It says that the Pied Piper stole all of our fish and traded for riches!" he said taking the newspaper he'd brought with him and showing it to his wife.

She looked at him with her mouth wide open in disbelief.

"And how do you know it wasn't that vile fat pig that governs us?" she argued.

"He's also taken people's money before! And poisoned the river in order to leave the town without any fish. It's all been published in the paper woman!"

"Only you would believe what that bitter Lez writes," she countered.

"Talk about pouring a bucket load of salt into sour wounds! The Mayor is to blame for all this mess." The fisherman's wife collected the potatoes one by one and tossed them in a pot of boiling water.

"Whose side are you on anyway?" the fisherman grumbled. "We should all unite against a common enemy, not squabble amongst ourselves. All this philosophy will not return our children to us, nor will it fill our bellies. We have no food, nothing, and here you are making excuses for that brute again! I sometimes wonder if he stole your wits at the same time as our daughter."

"How I wish the Pied Piper had taken you instead of my child," snarled his wife while glaring at him with her arms crossed, as dinner cooked over the open fire.

***

The sun was setting, and the streets were already dark under the indigo sky. Households had lit their candles as they ate dinner. Snowphia had just finished her shift for the day at the prison. She adjusted the scarf draped over her honey-coloured locks and fastened a cloak around the collar of her linen blouse. On her way home, she always passed through the fish market in the middle of the town in case there was any fresh fish about. It has been months since her family had last eaten a decent meal.

"How is your poor mother?" asked one of the market traders.

"Mama is coping - at least she has Christmas to look forward to," Snowphia replied, with a hint of concern showing through despite her usual optimism.

Her mother had relapsed back into another depression. Ever since she'd lost Maddie, her oldest daughter, to the Pied Piper, she hadn't been the same. Snowphia's mom, Mrs. Blumenthal, had started talking to herself again. Snowphia hoped that it wouldn't get any worse, lest she has to leave her job at the prison and care for Mama.

"Any fish today? I know Mama would love a good fish soup."

"Sorry my dear – not a single fish from the River Wesser, and you know who cursed it!" sighed the woman. "But we have worms if you don't mind trying something new - they are selling well, and I can give you a good price now that I'm closing!"

"Thank you for the offer, but I don't think that would suit Mama right now," Snowphia politely declined, trying to hide her queasiness at the proposition. "I'll just have some of that bread." She pointed to a stale loaf that was already greening with mould.

"Take it for free my dear - tell your mama it's from me."

"Oh, that's kind of you, thank you." Snowphia nodded in gratitude and placed it in her basket.

As she left the marketplace, two large, glossy black birds caught her attention. They pecked viciously, looking as if they were fighting. As she approached them, intrigued by the scene, she realised they were looking for food. They continued to hop about, nibbling at the pavement. Feeling sorry for them, she cracked off a piece of the stale bread and tossed it to the ground for them. The spectacle caught the attention of a group of young boys playing nearby.

"What do you think you are doing?" the tallest one demanded, pointing at the birds with his bony hand. A couple of the boys, shorter and more mischievous, ran towards the two ravens. The birds nervously flapped their wings and flew away.

"That could have been our dinner!" one of the boys shouted, as he gave up chasing the birds who'd taken refuge on a rooftop. The tallest of the boys reached down and seized the loaf of bread, taking a desperate bite into it before he divided the rest among his friends.

"Are you going to give us the rest of the bread, since you were happy to waste it on those stupid birds?" he taunted Snowphia.

She ignored them and tried to cross the street but they blocked her.

"I said give me the rest of the bread," said the taller boy, who crossed his arms to intimidate her.

"They looked hungry and I just wanted to give them something little to eat -"

Before she could say another word, another of the boys tore her basket from her and the group ran off. Only one of them lagged behind, discovering a pool of white goop dripping from his blond hair. One of the Ravens had pooped on his small lopsided head.

"I am going to kill those birds!" he shouted, taking off his shoe and hurling it towards the bird.

He missed, and the shoe went through one of the houses and landed at a family's dinner table causing a mess.

"Come on! Let's run for it," shouted one of the boys at his friend who was still lingering behind the group.

They all disappeared down the drumless street, the street supposedly the missing children were last seen.

CHAPTER 4

LONELINESS

Last night, I didn't get much sleep.

I was kept awake in anticipation of the news from Sherbert and Pepe. I was hoping they hadn't taken another jovial vacation and would come back with yet another dreadful greeting picked up from lord-knows-where.

I try to imagine what the young woman looks like, hoping she's like a princess – beautiful cascades of hair, a smile to penetrate my soul, and a kind heart that has the power to love unconditionally.

Well - a kind heart would do me just fine. Or the same taste for bean jar that I have, for that matter. I hear a rapping at the kitchen window. It's a double arch with three rows of grilles dividing each one, framed by two wooden shutters open at either side. I had the kitchen remodelled when I first settled in the house, just to give it a more "modern" look. Arches are so in style these days, I told myself. Oh, dammit! I cleaned the windows yesterday and forgot to open them this morning. Just then, I hear a thump to the glass.

Ouch! Sherbert has smashed himself into the glass!

"Did you clean your windows AGAIN without bothering to leave them open?" he chides, a little dazed from the accident. He wiggles his tail feathers irritably. "I swear, Pepe, this is the last time I do errands for him!" Sherbert tries to lift his wing but is in too much pain to do it completely.

"Is it bad?" Pepe asks. He examines Sherbert's feathers and then shakes his head. "Can't see a thing, to be honest. – Ah, here comes the guilty fellow."

"Arghhh, what do you have to say for yourself, sir? You know very well that we don't take very kindly to such petty attempts to punish us." Sherbert complains, cringing as he tries to lift his injured wing again.

"Well, I'll think to be sorry once you bring me some good news!" I tell them. I'm in no mood for morning pleasantries. I've lived with these two long enough to know that if I apologize, they'll milk it for all it's worth.

"Tell me you found another beautiful damsel, perhaps in the kingdom of Africa or even Mongolia?" I beseech.

"Well, we didn't bother with Asia, as it's freezing out there…and it's the rainy season in Africa, so there weren't many attractive girls hanging outside when we were around that's for sure."

"Oh!" I say, trying to hide my disappointment.

"Well, if you hadn't tried to get me KILLED, I would have told you how much fun we had yesterday," Sherbert interrupts.

"You had fun while I stayed all alone? Perhaps I should clean my windows every night."

"So, maybe you should, considering you are going to be alone for a very long time!" Sherbert snaps back.

"Touché!" He's always been mouthy, and more occasionally, he tries to show me who's the boss.

"Well, if you are really serious about finding someone, you ought to go for the girl we found you in Hamelin."

"She is definitely a beauty," Pepe affirms. "So beautiful that we don't even know whether she's married or not. But we kept an eye on her all day, and she doesn't seem to have anyone."

"Did you look elsewhere across Europe or even the North Pole?"

"Keep in mind it's only two of us against the millions of beautiful maidens all over the place. Plus, we don't even get paid for this, Mr. Piper!"

"Instead of pay the Pied Piper, it really should be, pay the Ravens, eh?"

"We meditated for a few days and then followed the wind. Our instincts told us to head back to Hamelin."

That always gets me. Their instincts are always right and always have been. Without their knack for knowing exactly where to look, I don't think I could have earned half the wealth that I've acquired as a Piper. Even if they hadn't bothered to look elsewhere, the fact that the winds point towards Hamelin is enough to convince me to go along with it. Though perhaps, I want them to show me that they've really tried their best.

"Erm," Sherbet interrupts, as he sees me ruminating on the situation.

"Well, do you want to hear what happened or not?"

"What?" I shake my head, pulling my mind back to the matter.

"So, about your young lady, she was kind enough to feed us some bread."

"Aww," Pepe chimes in, swaying from side to side in exaggerated affection.

"I mean, we had to pretend to be in distress and on the brink of starvation," Sherbert adds, his eyes animated. He loves telling stories. It's hard to believe that this bird gifted with such cleverness has just clumsily crashed into my window. "And she came over to us and gave us a big chunk of bread - I mean, it was stale and mouldy but -"

"Well, it's the thought the counts, right?" Pepe interjects. "Then some boys tried to bully her for it."

"They had the cheek to chase after us for their dinner…"

"What is it with humans and wanting to eat everything that moves?"

"I mean, who eats ravens?" Pepe adds.

"We then flew onto the roof just to keep watch. So, they turned to your, erm, future missus, and tried to steal the remaining loaf of bread from her."

"Funny enough, at that moment I felt the – sudden urge to poop…"

"Oh, you didn't." My eyes widen, sure of what was coming next.

"Oh, we BOTH did!"

***

"Thank you all for coming." I give the best smile I can, considering the circumstances, glancing at each one of my animal friends standing before me in the drawing room.

"Oh, did we have a choice about whether or not to come?" Chuka the monkey asks cheekily, clearly not keen on waking up for the meeting I've called for.

"Shush," the giraffe scolds, tilting her never-ending long neck towards him.

All I can do is purse my lips and nod. Sarcastic remarks are inevitable with this bunch.

"Thank you." I scratch my head, gathering my words. "Look, it pains me to admit this, and I do not mean to offend anyone."

All eyes become firmly fixed on me. Their facial expressions look like they are expecting some terrible news.

"It's not as bad as you might think but still kind of bad," I confusingly try to reassure them.

"It's just that… I'm thinking of-"

"Leaving us for good!" Coco chimes in.

I hold out my hand, gesturing for her to quiet down. But I know it's impossible with friends like these.

"Of late you haven't been coming out to the Candie garden, nor even just checking in on us," she complains.

"Just say it, you're fed up of this Guernsey animal farm and you want to leave us and go back to wherever you came from!"

Funny how they are the ones always worried about my leaving. If only they knew I'm a wanted man back at Azwan, they wouldn't be thinking I'm eager to go back there. If I ever set a single foot back in that land, I'm going to run into big trouble.

"W-wait a minute," I stammer. "Is that how everyone else feels? After all I've done for you guys - you really think I would just up and leave?"

I take a seat on my favourite wooden engraved chair, hoping it will calm me down.

"T-that I'd leave and go where? I am the most wanted man in the world right now - there is a big bounty on my head."

"I can't go back to my real home," I say sadly. My gut churns at the idea of going back to where I'm prone to die at the hands of those who were once my people. A look of relief passes through their faces.

"You owe me piggybacks around the island," one of the deer whispers to Coco. It turns out, they've made a bet about whether I am leaving or not.

"Just like you lot, I would like someone to be here with me. A human friend. Look at you all - you are in pairs as if we are heading for Noah's ark any day now; you have each other. As for me - I have no one."

"Aww," one of the lionesses coos. The rest of the animals stare at her in ridicule, until her dreamy smile droops in embarrassment.

"Why didn't you tell us before?" Coco asks me.

"Well, I've been riddled with guilt my entire life, but I just can't bear to be alone anymore. I mean, I enjoy all your company, I love playing with you guys - but I just want more…"

"Not trying to shatter the lovey dovey mood here and be bossy and all, but I usually sleep all day. Are we going to get somewhere with this?" Leo, the only male lion on the island, demands.

"Just ignore him," Mango, the lioness, jumps at my defence.

"See, I asked Sherbert and Pepe to go search for a wife for me. They've found someone – the perfect woman, actually - but there is one little problem. She's in Hamelin!"

The room falls deadly silent. "Ah, so its not only me who thought this was a deathly idea then!" I sarcastically remark while side eyeing the ravens.

"Oh no…" Chuka mumbles.

"Can we not just go steal a human from one of the nearby towns or something?"

"I heard the women there have beautiful, long hair and a smile that could light up this entire room. Can you imagine this place if you had such wonderful company?" says Chuka in a dreamy voice.

The nearby town indeed has beautiful women, but they're quite reserved and mistrusting of strangers that attempt to cross their borders. It's very unlikely they'll welcome the infamous Pied Piper!

I think thoroughly if finding a woman to be my soulmate is worth it, and I come to the realization that, if I want to survive, I can't go around stealing women. Besides, who would want to be stolen? This will end up Hamelin all over again! I'm going to be blamed all the same. People will judge me for my past, just like the people of Hamelin. But what's better, to be known as a child thief or women stealer? Give me a women any day with a bit of that Stockholm elixir to work its magic, eh!

"If we do that, I'm risking punishment from the law. I don't think you want me to be jailed any more than I want to go to jail," I say, glancing around the room to look at my companions.

"I can't cause any problems here or, soon, I'll find myself without a place to live again."

"It's bad enough that I am wanted for stealing kids from Hamelin, and you're telling me to go and steal a woman from another random town?"

"Fair enough."

"Perhaps go in disguise?" Oscar the chameleon proposes, while his scaly skin changes from rusty red to magenta and then to blue as he speaks. He always has been a nervous wreck hence the random colour changes giving away his nervousness.

"Good thinking," Coco peeps.

"But go as what?" I ask them.

"Maybe a circus man?" Chuka suggests, probably inspired by the fact that I rescued him from a circus once upon a time.

I rub my chin. "I can see myself doing that, but I'm not really much of a juggler."

"Or maybe go back as yourself, the Pied Piper, it will be like the second coming sort of thing," Trigger, the donkey innocently proposes. Chuka covers his face in shame.

"Tell you what - I am now convinced more than ever that, we are all equal but some of us are more equal than others," mocked Chuka as he shook his head in disbelief.

All the animals are fond of Trigger, but by god is he stupid! From a very young age, Trigger has always been slower than his kin. Donkeys are known for being stupid, but, judging by their very low standards, even his family, felt that he had inherited a fair share of that stupidity more than others. I met him when he was a sad and ostracized donkey from his family. He was the youngest of his siblings. Raised like the rest of them but with a kinder heart and a difficulty to understand what he should and shouldn't say. Tired of being always left out and mocked by his family he left and mistakenly followed me all the way here. It's a shame he takes all the credit for getting to this place, but he doesn't know half the story!

The other donkeys have soon realized that talking to Trigger requires a great deal of patience. Whenever he is asked something, he's often prone to understand everything the opposite way of what the interlocutor meant. For example, if he is asked to repeat something he has said, he repeats the last words he uttered and, when he is asked to repeat the words that came before those, he can't understand.

When he came to us, seeking friendship and a family to love him, I accepted him. And now he is making a stupid suggestion out of goodwill. All the animals complain loudly. I chastise them with a stern look. They know he can't help it. Trigger casts me an innocent look and I give him a small smile.

"Anyone else has any idea?" I ask, looking at my companion's curious faces.

There's a murmur and a strange cough and, when I raise my eyes to meet my interloper, I find Bolt looking at me with a mischievous glint in his eyes. I already suspect he is behind the ruckus, but I can't always blame him without any proof.

Bolt finally exclaims excitedly:

"You could go as the Prince of Sheba!"

My mouth opens to counter this idea, but right now I can't think of a better idea to tackle this situation. If I go there, I could be at risk of getting caught, but if I don't…Let's just say I don't want to be here for the rest of my life all alone.

"You could wear a beautiful attire! Make it stand out to the rest of the world without it screaming you're the world-famous Pied Piper!" says Bolt.

"Why wouldn't he want to be known? He's a personality! People like charming personalities like his," says Trigger slowly. He clearly is taking this seriously than most, poor Donkey! There's a collective groan and I must explain firmly, but in a kind manner, that I'm only getting in trouble if they know who I am. Trigger nods slowly. He sort of gets it or not!

"I meant that he was a Prince before being known as an animal charmer," says Bolt flashing a slightly condescending look at Trigger. "He could dress himself as the Prince of Sheba and none would be the wiser to his other identity."

I picture it. Me dressed in a regal attire. With my distinguished good looks, I'll look handsome, and no one would dare to dispute my heritage. It's a truth with a touch of lies. Sometimes you have to do the best you can with the things that life throws at you.

I raise my eyebrows. "Eureka!" With a conclusive nod, I stand up, ready to put the plan into action. "So, who will come with me?"

They all look in every direction but mine.

"Uh, I need to go pee," one of the animals whines as she heads towards the door.

"I also need to pee badly," another one adds.

A few more of my pets exit one by one. Am I disappointed? Yes. But I'm not surprised. They have had their fair share of bad experiences with humans, and the last thing they want to do is go back to that world again.

"I don't mind going since they can't eat me," Chuka offers, shrugging his shoulders. I look at my unicorns, Storm and Bolt, and they, noble to a fault, give me a determinate look.

"I'll come with you," says Bolt and he moves a hoof in a friendly gesture.

"I'll go with you too. Always count me in for anything dangerous, I'm not like those babies," he says, referring to our other companions. "Besides," he says quietly, "they're about as trustworthy being secretive as good ole Trigger. They just believe they're better than him but sometimes they're slower than him!"

I look around, worried that poor Trigger will hear us, but he's nowhere to be found. He's probably gone to pee too or eat.

"You just have to go back there with us and make it seem as if you're taking a tour with your magical companions instead of a magical escape," says Bolt. He gives me a reassuring look and nods to himself.

"I guess I'm too young and small to come, but I wish I could," I hear Boris say from the table in the corner of the room.

His pedipalps tremble, and he's seemingly on the verge of tears. He knows I'll have to leave him alone for some time while I go on my journey. Coco hurries over to him, comforting him with a few nuzzles of her shiny nose. I walk over to my loyal pets and hug them one by one. As for the ones who've left already, I don't blame them for being cowards – sometimes I feel like one too. But I could never thank the rest of them enough for sticking by my side at such a crucial moment in life. I know if I get in any trouble, they will do anything to help me.

I sit by them with my special flute. It's made of the same material with the one I played to enchant the animals, but this one emits a warm melody that has a melancholic tune to it. I don't plan on these melodies; they just come from the deepest corners of my soul, and I pour all my soul in it as my pets slowly start coming to rest by my side.

The next sound is a slow transition from a dry tone to a rich one that I drag for a few minutes. My pets have their eyes closed, enjoying the rhythm and, by the open window, the wind blows slowly; nature's way of matching my time with its own. I close my eyes and start playing the flute. I think of how we came here together and how I've felt loved and understood by companions in a way I haven't felt with my own kin. The sweet serenade stretches with the wind and, with my friends as company, I find the motivation I need to go ahead with my plan.

My friends seem to feel the same way. I notice their anxiousness slipping from the room, and all the animals seem to relax as I finish the final notes. I glance around and give a warm look to Boris whose eyes are half-lidded, and I smile as I think of how loyal and valiant he is. I know little Boris will never let me down, no matter how the others reacted. Though, I am not sure how much help he is going to be in the plan, besides acting as some child-like innocent moral support. Nevertheless, if I take him there, it will be risky. I don't want to jeopardize his safety (or any of the other animals' for that matter). The truth remains that I feel comfortable with them by my side, but I can't be stationed here forever. However, if I get caught, I'll die alone in Hamelin.

It isn't an easy decision and I wish I could have a support, someone to help me decide. However, making my own decisions is part of what makes me a resilient person and I want to transmit this resilience to someone someday. Once I think about the possibility of being caught, I can't get it out of my head. Wondering what could happen is one of my problems, I tend to forget about enjoying the present moments.

What has happened to the calming sound of waves lapping against my boat that usually lulls insomniacs like me to a peaceful night's slumber? The price of redemption from guilt increases day after day. I am sure it will turn me into a mad man in no time.

So, how am I to rid of this guilt? To complain is to cry over spilt milk. Out alone at sea with Fatso for company – that is the best I can do to seek some solace. Fatso is one of the rats that were once considered a pest problem in Hamelin. I was, technically, hired to get rid of them, and, that I did.

The townspeople of Hamelin firmly believed I was luring rats to their deaths at the River Wesser, but instead I had other plans for the little cute creatures.

After striking the deal with the people of Hamelin, I came to the rats and presented them with a simple offer: come with me and I won't harm you, with only two simple conditions and they'll be free. I offered them a place by my side, protection in exchange of their companionship and respect.

One of my conditions was that they always had to be clean, and now here is Fatso cleaning himself in one of my unused cups. He's washing his little face, scrubbing thoroughly underneath it and then, moving to his arms and small paws. He looks as if he is mentally debating by himself too. His small features are twisted into a serious mask that's a little unlike him.

The other condition I asked for him (and his kin) was much simpler: he needed to be happy and keep others happy. He's looking rather mournful at the moment, but I'll take his cleanliness as a good sign.

Everyone, the people of Hamelin and the rats accepted the deal – and both would be happy.

I just had to make sure that the cacophony of sounds emitted from the rats would never be heard no more, or else we would opening a large can of worms or rats, dare I say!

The rats naturally liked living in a group. They had a natural sense of what we know as living in a community. These small pets loved playing around each other and demonstrated affection easily, but one of them was an exception.

Fatso, however, is a quiet, solitary fellow. He enjoys being alone, unless he is around me. Fatso loves showing me affection and listening to my music. I've never asked him why he prefers my company, but I appreciate it at any rate. I give him a look before commenting on my thoughts.

"Whose universal moral standard have I violated so much that I am tormented every day?" I wail. Fatso just ignores me, offering me nothing more than a blank stare. Maybe he too is thinking of abandoning me along with all my problems. There's only so much mourning a rat can take in its short lifetime.

I've skipped my usual bread and pickled cabbage for breakfast. I'll have my favourite bean jar later tonight if I get my appetite back. My deep thoughts occupy me too much to make me want to do anything useful with my time. Sometimes I wish I was more like my animal friends. Being the avid opportunist, omnivorous eater, that he is, Fatso never worries too much about his next meal. Anything is edible for him. Clothes, shoes, wood, metal, you name it – if he can sink his little teeth into it, its fair game!

I continue to stare into the deep blue expanse of the sea, enraptured by the cool, still morning waters. It's as if I'm waiting for my reflection to say something back to me.

"Redemption!" I mutter to myself with a bitter laugh. I shake my head in amazement. "What a strange thing. Who should be seeking atonement for their soul?" Fatso looks up to me. Maybe it's the fact that he, the only of my pets who doesn't speak, can't argue with me. I have no fear in confiding to him. "Me, as the wronged party who performed a fair task for a fair payment. Or those who did me wrong? I played the game by their rules and yet I'm the one they call guilty!" ""I'm now the infamous PIED PIPER!"

Fatso wiggles his nose, either his way of agreeing with me, or telling me to shut up.

"My conscience is clear," I affirm, taking a deep breath, fixing my gaze back out into the waves of clear water that flux and flow in front of the distant hills.

"Aren't we all relieved to hear that!" says a plummy voice from underneath the boat.

"We were beginning to wonder what a miser we have here for company!"

"That's harsh," I snap back to the mystery voice.

"Look, I need something from you."

I look around the boat. I find nothing. It's just Fatso who's curiously watching my every movement. I'm usually out here all alone.

"Why bother to look for me?" the voice inquires.

"I represent free creatures. We are everywhere, and yet nowhere, and you will see only what you are ready to see. For now, you must only listen. Use your ears and heart as opposed to relying on the visceral comforts of your eyes."

I look to the left.

To the right.

Upwards to the azure sky.

Around the boat.

I turn to Fatso.

He squeaks to protest his innocence.

"Oh, dear me," sighs the voice.

"Who are you? What do you want from me?" I choke.

Am I dreaming? Perhaps it is time for me to leave Guernsey. Maybe all this time alone is starting to take its toll on my mental health. Talking to animals is one thing. But to hear voices and constantly have nightmares is something else!

"How 'bout I bring you some of the finest and rarest gems from under the sea - Poudretteite, Benitoite, Red Beryls…Oh, Painite, you will love those…and Taaffeites, Jadeites…?"

"STOP! STOP! Just stop talking," I interrupt, throwing my hands on my head. "What do you want from me?"

"Worms," blurts the voice in reply.

My mouth falls open.

"Any earthworm will do just fine. As long as they smell nice and wiggle – we are in business my friend!" sings the voice.

"L-let me get this straight," I stammer. "You want earthworms?"

"Nightcrawlers, if I may be specific."

"Yes, yes, yes - you want nightcrawlers in exchange for gems?" I laugh under my breath.

"Yes!" sings a chorus of voices.

It seems I have more company than I first thought. But this time around, it is comforting to know that at least I am getting the best end of the bargain. A better bargain than what Hamelin offered last time around! Or so I think. The spark of joy is short-lived though, as I realise, I have no use for the gems.

"The gems will make you a very wealthy man, sire - more than any purse of gold coins one could ever hope for." The voice seems to read my mind. "You will become the most eligible bachelor in the land. With so many gems, you can at last find a soulmate to soothe your troubles."

"For a moment there, I thought you would suggest me a wife," I muse as I recline in my small rowboat. "A soulmate, though? Th-that changes everything. You have my attention mystery voice of the sea."

"I'd prefer you know me as the Sea Captain but that is neither here nor there. What matters is you keep your end of the bargain, and we keep ours. And believe me when I say this, unlike the Mayor of Hamelin, who lied through his fat neck and cheated you of your thousand guilders - we will pay your gems upfront."

"How do you know about the ---?" I sit up, growing uneasy.

"Well, you always talk in your sleep about what happened in some place called Hamelin," murmurs the voice.

"But they cheated me first!" I snap back. "I didn't receive a single guilder that was owed to me! Was I to allow this, and not get revenge? I have my reasons for what I did!"

"And yet, despite being adamant that you are the wronged party, it is you who ends up out here all alone. No offence to the rat. But you seem to be lonely and always talking to yourself." The voice chuckles with an air that verges between pity and mockery.

"We were actually having second thoughts about making a proposal thinking that you may be a lunatic!"

"Considering I am talking to an invisible voice, perhaps I have lost my mind," I huff, suddenly self-conscious that I may be talking to only the guilt that swims around in my head.

Yet, the suggestion that I am lonely pierces my heart and catches me off guard. It starts to dawn on me. I am aware that I have acted every bit as dishonourably as the Mayor and his cronies. But my pride still won't let go.

"Whoever you are - I can assure you, you do not know the full story," I protest. "My side of the story has never been shared, and I am disinclined to share it with an invisible judgemental voice."

"Well, if you had a little faith and looked into the waters, you would have known that you were talking to a rather clever fish."

I slide to the edge of the boat to have a look. Down below, in the clear waters, I catch sight of a shoal of fish.

"Hello there - I am Spinky," a small clownfish introduces itself. It is a bright iridescent orange with three white stripes, like a tiny, glowing tiger. He swims closer to the boat, as the rest of the group disperse off into the distance.

"All along, had I known I was speaking to a clownfish?" I ask in disbelief.

"Oh, are we playing the fish card again?" Spinky teases.

"A talking spider or deer doesn't surprise you, but a talking fish does?"

"I'll ignore the fact you are pulling rank again!"

"Out here, we are all equals because we are all free!" Spinky insists.

"I know. I just didn't expect this kind of wit and bartering from you," I groan, rolling my eyes.

"Have you kept quiet to lure me into a false sense of security?" I exclaim to Fatso, who just wiggles his nose at me.

"Maybe he can't talk, sir," Spinky chimes in. "And perhaps having to make a deal with a bunch of politically correct disembodied fishes may stretch our credibility with you, but you will get used to the idea, that I am sure."

Maybe it's my mood, but I feel bad for having been defensive with the little, cheeky creature. "Look, sorry for getting angry at you earlier," I say.

"No worries, matey. The fact is, you tell yourself that you are happy here; that you have found your Utopia. It's safe out here but when you close your eyes, Piper, and search within your heart, are you free of the guilt? Are you free or do you tell yourself comforting lies to avoid questions from within that may lead to uncomfortable answers?"

"Either you are talking so much sense right now or I am a stark drunk alcoholic Pirate hallucinating terribly!" I reply half-jokingly.

What do I have to lose? I have a free therapist right in front of me. How he's managed to acquire so much wisdom under the sea, though, is beyond me.

"The thing is, I do not feel guilty for what I did, but perhaps for how I went about it. Each night I am tormented, not by guilt, but by not telling my side of the story. Although people can forgive, they never forget. For the rest of my days and beyond, I shall be the "child snatcher," or the "child killer" - the Pied Piper who took away Hamelin's children. My presence there will never be welcomed. It's impossible to try to explain something like that to any parent." I shake my head sadly. "You can try to make them forget. It's never too late," Spinky suggests.

"Make peace with yourself, matey. That's what us sea-dwellers have done for years."

I frown, not quite understanding. "What do you mean? Why do I fear I'm about to receive a lecture that will make me question my life choices? Something that will force me to confront my fears and stop making excuses for my unhappiness?"

"For many years, humans, or as you sometimes call them, Earthlings, have hunted, killed, and eaten my kind. I have lost many friends and family to their greed. It has wounded and hurt me; it would have been easy to lose hope. Thankfully, we discovered this place and are now free - even though our freedom came at the price of us not having worms anymore. We couldn't help but follow you when you brought your rat friends here! The call to your music was too strong," says Spinky.

"But how did you get here in the first place? I didn't see you following us," I say as confusion starts to give way to some realisation of what is going on, "...we came by earth and you can only swim!"

"We found ourselves swimming through a space we've never seen before. It seemed to stretch out forever, endlessly, until we landed here with the rest of you of lot"

My gut twists and turns as I realise the cause of Hamelin's latest troubles. In Hamelin, there's a beautiful woman that could potentially become my wife, and my friends need to eat worms that I can only find there. However, the fact remains that I am now to blame for both the disappearance of the missing children of Hamelin and its food troubles, and now the town's a mess and I am considered a Public Enemy. I drop my head.

"I just want to know how I can get some peace?" I implore, suddenly on the verge of tears. I suddenly regret ever choosing to help Hamelin in the first place. Asia had been kinder to me.

"Just like us, you humans, or whatever you call yourselves, give birth. I hear it is a more painful experience for your womenfolk, judging by the screams and screeches we often hear, I'll give them that, but here is my point. If we were to ask one of your womenfolk if they'd like another child during the throes of labour, they would snap at us and call us many foul names known under the sun. BUT, as if by some magic, as soon as the tiny human is within its mother's arms, the tiny thing casts a little spell on its mother and all pain is soon forgotten."

"But how can I, the child thief, make the people of Hamelin forgive or even forget after what I did to them?" I ask in despair.

"That, my, dear friend, you will have to figure it out on your own," is all Spinky said before turning away from the boat and drifting back out into the ocean. Before going too far, he stops in his tracks and looks back at me.

"I know you are all emotional and all - but are we still good for the worms? I mean if push comes to shove, I can see to it that I arrange a deal with some of the mermaids under hear and all – but only if you not up for it, with all this self-pitying it looks more than likely – but are we still good for the worms though?"

Spinky isn't keen on letting all this emotional talk get in the way of some serious business ahead. A shimmering treasure chest suddenly appears, floating, right at in the spot where Spinky was. It's already open, with a royal blue velvet drawstring bag inside it. But what will I do with all those gems? A glimpse of the shiny stones distracts me from the conversation.

"Is this how all you people cope with loneliness and despair?" Spinky asks as he perches his mouth above the waters to take a breath. "Busy fantasising about a better life but doing nothing about it? Look at us Mr Piper, instead of fantasising about the invisible ocean and bemoaning the lack of safety found in the open sea, we spent many years and acted in great sacrifice until we found it. By the time we did, we were safe and secure in the knowledge that we'd earned our freedom."

I take a moment to muse upon his question, wondering whether I should take offence. Maybe it is time for me to be as wise as he is and reply with some level of calmness.

"I consider loneliness to be both a blessing and a curse," I conclude.

"It is a blessing because, in that moment, time appears to stop. It's just yourself and your thoughts –imagination can take you anywhere you wish to be, as the very version of yourself that you consider the best. No judgment. No prejudice. Loneliness has been my friend since I came here, but a selfish friend one at that. It wants you, and you alone to itself. Over time you become awkward to the rest of the world. You grow selfish and find that the company of others cannot measure up to the standards set by your own."

Spinky flutters his fins as if clapping at my eloquent monologue.

"That all went past my fins but sounded deeply wise and a tiny wee bit dramatic."

I am impressed with my own perceptiveness. I look into the distance in silence, perhaps just for the dramatic effect.

"I am content alone, but I would be happy with somebody at my side. What I have observed in life is that there are people who are lonely and alone, and others that are alone but not lonely. On the other hand, there are people who are lonely in company, but also people who are surrounded by others and free of loneliness."

Spinky flutters his fins again. "Bravo, Mr. Piper. Those are some deep thoughts to share with a so-called talking fish, eh? You should write them down on a scroll or something. Now, if only I knew where to find mermaids, I'd have put in a good word for you." He chuckles to himself. I didn't even know fish could make that sound too, but then, again, he is a talking fish or the talking Sea Captain as he pompously calls himself.

"But in the meantime, if I may offer some advice, it sounds to me that there is a void in your life that can only be filled by another human being or something with spiritual power."

"Exactly, "I sigh. "I feel it, deep down inside. When I am alone is when I feel the darkness."

CHAPTER 5

LONDON

The sun shines brightly through the arched frame of glass, causing me to squint my eyes. This time, I have left the windows open a crack, so Sherbert can't accuse me of plotting another accident waiting to happen. It also means they couldn't bother me before I am awake enough for a proper conversation.

"Rise and shine, darling!" I hear Sherbert's voice shout. "Today, we'll set off on our mission to win the heart of your future wife! Hamelin's finest."

I yawn, stretching my arms up. Just the thought of the mission ahead makes me want to stay in bed a few hours longer. "Right," I finally reply in my groggy morning voice.

"Don't forget we have to pass through London to get the stuff we need and all. Then we'll head to Hamelin – and maybe just die there!"

"I know, I know," Sherbert reassures me. Meanwhile, Pepe is picking up some breadcrumbs he's discovered from a crumbly day-old muffin next to an empty teacup.

"I take it you will be following us to London too?" I still can barely believe they'd go there considering how much they hate big European cities. They haven't quite figured out how to navigate with all the horses and carriages moving about.

"Eh, we'll see about that," Pepe replies, more interested in his own breakfast of muffin crumbs than anything else.

"Anyway, where is the rest of the gang?" I ask. If I were to guess, I'd say Chuka doesn't mind coming, because it's just another adventure for him and he doesn't mind discovering new places. It's the unicorns I'm worried about. They don't take too kindly to humans; it took years for them to even trust me. But one thing that makes the animal kingdom special is their willingness to try. Either they do not reason like we do, so they have no clue of the consequences, or they genuinely know what is happening but do not care. Maybe, it's that we look at death very differently. For them, it's an everyday part of life, considering you are born to be another animal's supper, whereas for us humans, it's something we hope to avoid for as long as possible.

Speaking of the unicorns. "Ah, there you are!" I greet them, as Storm and Bolt walk into the room. The rest of her crew are following behind. Good thing the animals do not need to pack, brush their hair, or get dressed before going out. They just come as they are and are ready to go.

As for me, I groom my messy dreadlocks and put on the finest tunic and breeches that I own. After all, I want to make a good impression in London, just in case the worm and gems plan falls through and I have to return to my usual job of charming pests with a flute.

I grab my djembes, which are especially designed to have a synthetic cover instead of animal skin. I acquired them on one of my trips and I haven't used them as much as I'd have liked to. I touch them with my hands, reaching across the worn, soft texture as a nice sensation overcomes my senses and I gather my audience's reactions. Like before, I feel their hesitation, laced with worry and fear and I give them a shaky smile.

"Do you want to hear me playing this? I wish I could play them more often," I say. The truth is sometimes I would like to think that I'm a powerful music magician, who often loses the feel of magic flowing through me as easily as it once did.

"However, the true reason why I'm so eager to play this instrument is that it allows me to make all traces to this island and the island itself invisible. No one will bother us this way," I say slowly.

Moments ago, they looked enthralled by the beauty of the instrument and now, some of them look surprised, but, Bolt and Storm (the smartest of my companions) nod. They understand the importance of the island being virtually erased from existence.

I start tapping the drums with my hands, eliciting the bass sound to drown out and my companions start to dance and laugh merrily.

I smile to myself as I watch them dance. The smaller ones move their heads or antennae, but the bigger ones move their anterior and posterior paws to match the movements I'm making with my feet. I move my arms and lean into my drums to raise the intensity of the tapping. Dragging the sound of the drum, I whistle along the rhythm and they start making sounds with their paws. Bolt looks excited as he wobbles around his horn and inhales, then he puffs breath out through his nostrils. He's vibrating with excitement and I feel him slowly relax.

"We're going to make it better this time friends. I know we can do this and come back to safety without problems," I say trying to sound cheerful instead of worried.

Some seem terrified while Bolt looks ready to burst from pent-up energy.

"I want you all to come here and stand very close to me," I say as I drag the last notes of the drums. "Magic here works excellent the closer you step to the drums," I say, raising my voice above the sound of the drums, and the animals come closer to me. "I'm sure it won't fail me, but I'm calling you to make sure it'll work fine. That way it won't use only my energy but some of yours too. Don't worry, it's only meant to light up the spark that gives way to magic. It won't hurt," I say as I see some apprehensive looks around the room.

I'm apprehensive too, but they don't need to know that. I sense the shift in energy on the air. It feels as if the world around us is rearranging its shape as I speak

"Wonderful!" I exclaim.

I carefully move next to them as I feel the magic slowly swirl around us with its invisible, but powerful presence. Magic, like animals and humans, is alive and both consumes, and produces energy. So, when it starts happening, I feel the slow creeping sensation of hot wind touching my skin, and the warm sensation gathers at the middle of the drums, where I'm touching them.

Storm looks at me alarmed.

"This is normal," I say, as my skin turns slightly red. "Now come, so we can make this happen."

They come closer and then I start instructing them:

"Alright," I turn to my pets with a nervous sigh. "A few rules before we jump in. Only I do the talking on this trip. If you speak, you risk exposing yourselves and spooking the humans into doing strange things to you."

They all nod in agreement.

"We're ready now to start with my new act of magic: taking us into London," I say shakily. Casting magic so powerful can be exhausting. "Prepare yourselves as I search for my flute," I say and, after rummaging through my things, I find the flute and start to play it.

Now, the magic feels cold. A shiver runs down my back and then gives way to something else, a thrilling sensation that rushes through each of my fingertips, all the way to the flute and back to my hands. I close my eyes and concentrate in the monotonous, almost sorrowful notes that open the portal by the wardrobe.

This isn't an exhausting task, not if it's compared with disguising an entire island with a magical cover blanket. This is easier to track too; it leaves a trail unknown by others but me. It clings to my skin after a while, almost like a fragrance, although it doesn't have any smell, but it gives me the sensation of being more noticeable and corporeal.

I remember that I haven't finished my explanation to them, so I cough nervously and start speaking again.

"If something happens to me, you stick with Chuka if you want to get home – you get that?" Chuka grins wide and proud. The unicorns nod in agreement again, but by the way they look at each other with trembling lips, I can tell they are apprehensive. Monkeys are known to be selfish in dangerous situations. After all, how else could you explain how Chuka made it to the island when he'd been part of a travelling circus?

"We will be heading to the big smoke first. It is plausible that I may have to leave you somewhere while I go and buy the items we need before we set off for Hamelin."

Storm's mouth drops open. "You are going to leave us all alone with Chuka in London of all places?"

"The English will find it awkward if they see me walking around the city with a couple of unicorns and a monkey," I try to reason. I can't deny though, I feel guilty that I may not be able to stay with them when they depend so much on my care.

"Look at it this way," I continue. "I'll bring you to a park where you can meet with other animals. And make new friends for life!" Storm's eyes light up. It's a relief to see her more inspired by the plan.

"Ok!" she agrees.

Fatso appears by my side; he's been waiting for my instructions and now that I'm ready to go, he gives me a hopeful look. I think about it briefly. Londoners won't take kindly to Fatso because his kind has a bad reputation already. After all, they had a horrible rat infestation not so long ago. His shining eyes regard me with a look that could persuade a heartless man. I caress his soft, shiny fur with my fingers, and he slowly closes his eyes. That does it. I realize I could easily take him there and have him hidden in a pocket without issue. Besides, he doesn't talk or make any sounds, and at least he's not as mischievous as Bolt and Chuka.

"Alright, you may come with me, my friend," I say quietly.

Fatso, Storm, Bolt and Chuka come closer to me. Fatso immediately hops in my pocket while the others stand at each side of me: Storm and Chuka on my left and Bolt on my right.

I roll the map open and place one of my hands onto it and play the flute with the other one to prompt our transport to the destination

I let Storm and others go through the wardrobe first. One by one, they disappear inside it. I wave goodbye to Sherbert and Pepe, who flap their wings towards me in response. I am hoping they do end up following us to London. "Good luck!" they exclaim, perhaps secretly wondering if they'll ever see me again. I take one last breath and jump in.

***

The snow gathers on the shoulders of my brown wool cloak. I tend to forget it's not springtime all year round in the rest of the world like it is in Guernsey. We nervously step into the busy London streets, and I quickly drag my companions out of the way of an incoming carriage.

I must think quickly of a special design for our chariot to use to roam around the city of London and beyond. And once I come up with the perfect idea, I start blowing my flute into a special melody.

The cartwheels start to form first. Next, appears the bronze reinforcements, which I shape into the shape of tan leaves Then comes the red velvet seat, which I make sure is spacious; I want to make sure people perceive us as high and mighty once we make an appearance.

Without me telling them, Bolt and Storm promptly move to the front of the chariot. I fasten the soft ties around them and, once everyone is in place, I caress the top of their heads, below their horns. "Let's go!" I say in a low voice, so only they can hear me.

Not surprisingly, people on the streets give our carriage a wide-eyed look. One of them, a beautiful woman with chocolate-brown hair, that was tied in the back in the form of braids and a long overflowing dress, looks at us and, before casting a small furtive glance around, she smiles at me briefly. I nod courtly and she looks away, back to minding her own business. It's the first sign of success for me and my distinguished attire! I suppose no one in London would have dared look at me admiringly if I was dressed in rags. As we go through the main city square in our carriage, we all can't help but watch all the elegant ladies with their embellished gowns and overflowing skirts, and the men with their pants held by suspenders of dark colours and bolder patterns such as plaid followed by a Victorian shirt in all sorts of colours.

"Welcome to London guys!" I say enthusiastically. They all look at me in horror.

"I'm sorry," I quickly apologize, shrugging my shoulders, as we glance around at the winter wonderland surrounding us.

We make our way to a nice leafy park. "I will leave you all here – make friends and play nice," realizing I better practice treating them like wild animals instead of friends, lest the townspeople lock me up for insanity. I pick up Chuka and prop him on my shoulder, as I hail a carriage to take us into the City's centre.

The main City square is alive with the hustle and bustle of activity. Women are passing by with baskets and flowing gowns brushing over the snow-covered ground. Accompanying them are men in their feather hats made of velvet and felt. All of them do a double take when they see me striding proudly with Chuka sitting on my shoulder.

"Do not move, you hear me," I whisper to him. "Only speak after I tell them that I am a ventriloquist." Chuka nods in agreement.

"Is that a real monkey you have over there, lad?" asks one of the men we were sharing the carriage with.

"No, sir. Do not let your eyes fool you my good sir, this is a stuffed monkey," I reply, exchanging a tight smile and a curt nod with my elegant interloper.

"Good Lord! And if I may ask, kind sir, and what are you doing walking around London with a stuffed monkey?"

"I am a ventriloquist," I say, waiting for Chuka to act his part.

"See. Only a good ventriloquist can make a stuffed monkey like me look and sound real," Chuka says in a high-pitched voice.

"Oooh mighty, mighty, I am impressed," the Englishman praises, excitedly clapping his hands. "Thank you," Chuka replies with a bow. I give him a pat to acknowledge his excellent, brief cameo.

We arrive at the main street lined with shops, right in the heart of London, and find just the place we are looking for: Hamleys.

The room is finely decorated in red and gold. I look at the high shelves overflowing with toys in all sizes and shapes. The options for girls range from life-sized dolls with curly hair and clear round eyes next to the elegant tea set with table and the skipping ropes, while boys have a line of marbles and toy soldiers to choose from.

There's an air of magic that I'm almost certain other people can feel it too once they enter the shop. There's waves of magical energy and love coming in and filling up the place, so much so that I can't help but smile candidly as I look at the array of colourful toys and think back to my childhood in Azwan.

"Welcome to the world's finest toy shop!" shouts a man with a thick moustache who is standing outside by the big doors behind us.

The shop owner looks up from the counter and examines me from head to toe, a bit thrown off guard to see the monkey accompanying me.

"Are you searching for something for yourself, sir? Or for your pet?" he asks me, raising one eyebrow curiously in Chuka's direction.

"Oh, no, no," I assure him. "It's a stuffed monkey. One of the most famous ventriloquist in all of Europe, actually." I was starting to impress myself with my ability to lie so skilfully.

"Indeed."

"Indeed, he is," Chuka says. "With a palace on a deserted island to vouch for it."

I click in frustration at the truth of his words but quickly draw a smile. Of course, nobody but me would know he was telling the truth!

"Bravo!" the shopkeeper praises. "Well, if I didn't know better, I would think that clever critter was real —"

"Dolls!" I exclaim, lifting my finger, eager to distract him from the thought about Chuka as soon as possible.

"I beg your pardon?"

"I need lots and lots of dolls. And puppets too. Chess boards. Bows and arrows. The whole lot. I have a festivity to attend, and the entire town's children are counting on it."

The shopkeeper suddenly beams, seeing that today was his lucky day - he'll make a fortune for sure thanks to the mystery rich ventriloquist in town! Every toy he points to, I nod to signal to him that I'll be purchasing. As he's packing the toys in a sack for me to transport, he looks up at me and says, "Will you be in London much longer, my good friend?"

"We are leaving tonight," Chuka squeaks.

"I'm mightily impressed how you keep in character!"

"Such a shame though. Her highness, the Duchess of Kent, is seeking entertainment for her Christmas celebrations and I'd put in a good word about you. You're the best ventriloquist I've seen yet."

"What we meant is that we'll be leaving, but will be returning later this month," I explain. "With a special guest, I should add."

"Splendid," the shopkeeper replies. "You'll be paid a handsome sum here for your talents."

"Earthlings and their promises!" I mumble to myself.

What amazes me is that everywhere I enter, I'm received with intrigue and applause. It makes me wonder if I should change my career altogether from a wandering Pied Piper to an honourable ventriloquist. I collect my custom-tailored Santa Claus suit from the costume shop.

Next stop is the carriage-maker, who offers me a stunning chariot accented with gold. I tell him I'll take it, not even thinking twice about the hefty price. I already made a chariot from my magic, but I'm in a happy mood, besides, I need to start spending in advance, the gems I will be getting from Spinky.

"You must be one very successful ventriloquist, alright," he comments, chuckling.

"I bet you earn a good wage as high as some of the most esteemed merchant bankers around here!"

"Tis true indeed! Practice makes perfect, and my commitment to the art has been rewarded," I affirm in a showy tone.

"Don't forget my commitment to the art," Chuka comments.

I merely smirk proudly. Mission accomplished – or at least the first bit. Now comes the challenging part, making our way to Hamelin with all these toys.

After grabbing the sack full of toys, I hail a carriage and instruct the driver to wait for me. The man is happy to wait seeing that London has welcomed one rich visiting ventriloquist!

I then look around, across the many stores and find the one I've been looking for all this time, the real reason why I came all the way from Guernsey to London: there in the beautiful chaos of incoming men, women and carriages there's a tall building with elegant lettering that reads 'De Beers'. I know my animal friends are growing impatient with me, but I need to make a visit to De Beers first. Then, maybe, we'll allow ourselves to have a tasty meal at the local open market.

Fatso finally musters up some courage, to take a peek outside from my pockets.

I enter the store and the store clerk immediately comes to my aid. He's dressed in a suit with long black coat, crisp white shirt, and black trousers. His shiny shoes make a steady dry sound against the wooden floor. He bends his head in greeting and I return the gesture.

"Hello, fine gentlemen, what can I do for you?" he booms in a gruff voice, while he can't stop himself from staring at Chuka.

"I came here looking for something special," I say.

His eyes glint with the possibility of a good fortune that awaits him. It's the perfect opportunity to make me buy something expensive. I would hate to be a pauper living in this expensive place!

"Of course, what were you looking for, sir?"

"I want the most beautiful pearls for a lady I'm going to court."

He hums thoughtfully, and then his eyes shine. "I have the perfect thing for you, sir." "Come, follow me this way. Mind your head!"

The man takes me to the glass vitrines where a wide array of jewellery is on display. As I admire the jewellery on display, I can't help but cast my mind back to what Spinky was offering me as an upfront payment of the finest gems in exchange of mere worms! Oh gosh, I start to panic and getting anxious. Maybe this whole going to Hamelin as some sort of rich Prince bearing gifts is one terrible idea!

"Sir, is everything okay?"

"Oh, I'm just amazed by the wide assortment of jewellery you have here!" I try to reassure the gentleman.

Some of the jewellery are big and shiny - some are tear-shaped, some in the shape of suns and moons and, some, are shaped like a small lotus flower made with encrusted diamonds. Others are small - a star-shaped necklace is placed on a special case next to a necklace with a butterfly pendant. However, I know the one I'm looking for is different.

As I look at the array of necklaces on display, I spot a beautiful almost magical pearl necklace. It was so simple and elegant, and yet I felt a tingle of excitement by the mere sight of it. The pearls shine and I can picture them enhancing the beauty of my future beloved. I don't know who she is or if she'd care for me, but I feel this could be an excellent addition to her style.

"That's the one," I say as I become breathless at the sight of the necklace once more. The man gently nods "You have a fine eye for exquisite jewellery. Very good choice my good gentlemen, I'll pack it for you in one of our special boxes. Anything else?"

"Maybe the matching earrings too?" I request with some excitement. The joys of shopping in hope for some love.

The man retreats to pack the pearl necklace and earrings, and I look at my hands, they're itching from touching the vitrine where the necklace was located. I hope it's a good sign.

"If I may, with your permission, can I tempt you with this bronze Pied Piper statue?" the man cheekily asks. The man is innocently looking to make a good fortune from me, but it doesn't stop my heart skipping a bit. The statue does resemble me slightly. Besides, how else could I afford all the toys and jewellery if it wasn't for my piping?

"No thank you that will be all!"

I hurry outside the store, with the box safely hidden in another one of my pockets. After a short walk away from the store, Fatso's head peeks from the insides of the other pocket and I pat his fur, signalling to him to remain calm. Thank goodness Fatso was on his best behaviour today.

He hides away as I enter the marketplace and start walking across it. There's a wide assortment of fruits and vegetables. I grab each of them in a copious amount (after all, I don't know when I'll be buying food again) and once I pay the seller, I grab my gatherings, and I signal for the man with the carriage carrying the toys I bought from Hamley's to give me a lift back to the corner of the street, near the park where the rest of my animal gang are surely impatiently waiting for me.

As I trudge through the snow, I'm overcome with sudden worry that I'll find Storm and the others shivering in the cold, alone and frightened.

I hear hooves in the distance. Not one animal, but many. As I approach the commotion, I find Storm and the rest of the unicorns chasing and nuzzling the reindeers that live in the park. The reindeers come near me and give Chuka and Fatso curious nudges. "I see you've made friends," I comment, as Storm runs over to greet me and Fatso. Bolt gradually joins her.

"It seems like we've made more friends now," Chuka jokes using his high-pitched ventriloquist voice.

"Oh, do we have to leave?" Storm whines.

The magical chariot reappears. I have a dilemma whether to take the one I magically conjured up using my flute or the golden chariot I just bought.

Bolt and Storm are so worked up from their game of tag that they run towards one of the chariots and hop on top of it. I guess my choice has been made for me. The Pied Piper's magical chariot it is! What a shame having to leave the other chariot back at the shop. Maybe I'll pick it up next time I'm back in London, to entertain the Duchess of Kent!

"Is everything alright?" asks Chuka excitedly.

"Better than alright. It's excellent!" I reply, proudly showing them the small special box with the pearl necklace.

Storm snorts and Bolt looks at me before neighing. They're both excited, but Storm seems more amused whilst Bolt is completely happy. Chuka squeaks, equally delighted and the silent Fatso looks at them with a glint on his sharp gaze.

"Alright, time for us to go," I say excitedly with a clap of my hands. Although the uncertainty of going back to Hamelin is making me uncomfortable. I shudder once more as I think back to the mini-nervous breakdown I almost had in the jewellery store.

"Come on, you two," I scold. "You're supposed to pull it, not ride it."

"Ohhh," Storm sobs. "Will we come back here… ever?"

"As a matter of fact, yes," I say. "I've been booked to give a ventriloquist show for some Duchess of Kent."

The group of unicorns explodes into ohs and ahs at the success story.

"Yayyy!" Storm replies. "I'm sorry. I didn't mean that I would let you down just to stay here. I know we came here to help you. Let me just say goodbye to our new reindeer friends and tell them that we'll be back."

After all my pet unicorns calm down from their day-long play session, I fasten their harnesses to the chariot, hoping they'll have enough energy left for the task. We carefully position the chariot in front of the tallest tree trunk we can find. The moonlight barely illuminates the sky through the flakes of snow that cloud the air. I dig my hands into my pockets, taking out the two magical stones, and lance them at the bark of the tree. Before I can even blink, we are suddenly pulled into the tree trunk.

CHAPTER 6

THE MESSENGER FROM AZWAN

A sudden gust brews, rallying a fresh flurry around us, making our throats groan and our skins crawl with goose bumps. True, we are in the heart of a forest. In the thick of winter. Much colder than it was in London! Yet, the rush of cold that comes knocking on our door, feels like an unexpected, uninvited visitor. Finally, the howling wind quietens, giving its billowing lungs a rest.

Few moments of stillness ensue. Then, through the muted rustle of unicorn hooves, comes another sound. A melody of trills, of bases and of everything in between. The notes drift through the sleet like snowflakes, and land by me. I recognise the tune; it is one that belongs to Azwan. But, from the shades and shapes of its notes, I can tell I do not know the music magician.

I listen on. The melody is lilting. Luring. And I decide to follow its path, tethered by the strong ropes of curiosity.

I'm the piper and I'm being lured. The irony!

"Are we not following the map?" Storm grunts, its furry brows crinkling at the shifting route.

"No, we are following the music," I admit.

Having left behind a mile of footprints in the woodland snow, we arrive at a long bridge. One whose ropes are frayed and whose planks haven't been trodden in decades.

The unicorns are unsure, but I am not. Storm and Bolt eventually drag their limbs forth, one hoof at a time. Chuka seals his eyelids shut, just as the carriage descends onto the bridge, the wheels rumbling from one unsteady plank to the next.

We manage to cross half the distance without any theatrics but our own dramatic reactions, when the structure trembles.

"What was that?" I yelp, my eyes scuttling from the left side of the steep drop to the right.

It moves again, and this time it is far more than a mere tremble; we're almost toppled towards the far side of the bridge.

"I have a terrible feeling about this!" I scream desperately.

They turn to me in unison, their beady eyes glowering.

"How comforting!" Storm scoffs. "This was your idea."

"Let's just head the other way?" Chuka proposes, his teeth chattering as badly as his nerves.

I look around, flustered. "No. Don't move!"

"Someone is doing this!" exclaims Storm surveying the bridge for the source of the upheaval.

"This isn't normal," I drawl, closing my eyes and concentrating my magic on the music and the spells flitting around the surrounding scenery. "Something, no, someone, a powerful music magician has enchanted this to act up against us," I murmur as my hands shake and my body freezes. "But who could this be?" I need a hint to understand the spirit – or, spirits - behind this.

"I like your reasoning, but I doubt that spirit will show up here," Storm nervously pulls on, resuming our perilous trek to the other end of the bridge.

The chariot creaks as we roll off the wood into the crunchy snow.

Suddenly, I notice a fuzzy silhouette behind the screen of falling snow. Actually, two fuzzy silhouettes. It takes us advancing a few wary yards before their solid forms crystallise on my eyes though.

"Woah," the unicorns stop in their tracks, growing restless in fear. Chuka latches onto my head for protection.

One is a white four-legged predator, a snow jaguar, posing on its haunches. Its fur, thick and shiny, is peppered with black spots. The two pale green eyes on its face, glitter like a pair of jades against the white. With eyes as sharp as that I imagine the canines its wide jaws are hiding might be deadlier than dagger blades. Brrrrr! I shiver, and not only because my veins are icing up.

Not far from the jaguar lingers the second silhouette, a lanky frame with two oversized fleshy ears jutting out, both as pointy as needle-tips. Its head is green and round, its forehead as wrinkled as crushed parchment. On top of its rotund head has sprouted a tuft of shaggy hair that I presume has never been introduced to a grooming brush.

I would have named the creature an elf – except for one glaring attribute that is not elf-like. A nose that glides all the way down to its waist, soft and leathery, resembling the trunk of an elephant. Odder still, the trunky nose meanders into several nostrils, each nostril a different size, each size denoting a different wind instrument. "A musical elf?" I murmur, recalling a folklore, though I cannot be certain of it.

"What are those... those things?"

The unicorns retreat a trot. Chuka's grip around my temple tightens so hard I am rendered a tad dizzy.

As two pairs of bulbous eyes stare at me, walking right into the walls of my soul, I can feel the colour on my skin pale. I decide to return to the carriage and head back, in the other direction.

Only to be drawn in again.

I turn around to leave.

However, I am back where I began. At this point, I am basically circling in my spot. "Damn!" I am slave to the compulsion of the musical elf's music.

"Who are you?" I decide to speak through the clatter of my teeth. "Can you talk?"

In a flash, the jaguar curls into a ball, inside which its form meshes into a lump, before reappearing as a fresh profile. One with a pair of hands, a pair of legs and a very human torso. He has penetrating emerald eyes and a dark, mystical visage, with a shiny bald head, framed with head jewellery that falls to his dark shoulders. His eyes glint with triumph.

"I knew it!" I punch my blue knuckles in the air. "I could tell something wasn't right about this place." I'm half-expecting the mysterious man to offer me an explanation, but he doesn't.

All he does is stand there, glaring at me in silence, as if ready to cast a spell.

I step closer to the mystery figures, approaching the duo for a better look.

"What do you want from me?" I demand. His stern face seems to emit nothing but unspoken disapproval.

"If you won't talk, then let us go our way," I demand, struggling to keep my voice steady.

"Greetings, master. The elf is Elvis." The musical elf speaks through one nostril, while continuing to belt out music through another - the pitch of its notes so perfectly tuned, our exchanges can't be overheard by Storm, Bolt, Chuka or Fatso.

"Your Majesty!" The man sneers and makes an exaggerated bow. He has a deep booming voice that makes me uncomfortable. It's at odds with his very human appearance.

I instantly dislike him. He reminds me of people back at home and the way he's addressing me confirms his heritage. Only another Nubian would call me that.

The realisation that I've been found by my kin hits me and then a number of things happen in quick succession. Fatso scurries out of my pocket, the animals holler. In the midst of the chaos, I make a cloud of smoke appear to take us somewhere afar.

I am pinched by guilt, but I can't let my friends know the truth.

The cloud, however, traps me with the man and the elf.

The man smiles crookedly, while the elf just... smiles.

"Ugh!" I wish I could get away with the things I want to do.

"Elvis serves the land you hail from. Elvis has been sent to let you know it is pointless to go to Hamelin." I'm briefly distracted by the manner in which the elf converses, as if it is addressing its own reflection in a mirror.

"Go back to Guernsey," the man adds calmly.

"Why would I go back when I have come this far?" I protest.

"Elvis is to warn you not to proceed, rather to serve your punishment until you are recalled."

"Do you know who you are? You are a Nubian prince and here you are prancing around like Santa Claus heading to a small town to find yourself a peasant woman. Acting like an Earthling!" His face contorts in anger.

"I quite like this outfit," I reply under my breath. He's as unreasonable as anyone back home is.

As unreasonable as they were back then.

I remember the last time I was in Azwan, and the court stared at me like I'd grown a tail.

I remember the way people would murmur as I walked in with a pet in my pocket.

They never got it. The way I am, the way I can be friends with my pets instead of submitting them under my thumb like all other humans do.

I hope this mission I'm going on isn't a waste of my time and I'll be able to find and build something real.

I don't want to go back to a place where I am a freak at worst and a mere puppet at best. I am no toy. I'm my own person.

I exhale and face them directly, keeping my mind in the present.

I wonder how they know about my plans.

"I order you to go back right now. Your father ordained your banishment, and you have not finished serving your time. You and your family will soon be reunited. We have already chosen a woman for you to protect the bloodline."

"Already?" I ask in surprise. "And where is this woman?" You could have let me know earlier and saved me from making this dangerous trip, I smirk to myself.

"Turn around and go back - you are on a fool's errand and you will only get this peasant girl into more trouble than it's worth."

"I have come this far, and I am not going back," I reply firmly, lifting my chin higher. "And I think you're lying, whoever you are."

"You think so? You will make her miserable. They're planning on taking more slaves - that girl, her family, her town, her country, no Earthling would be an exception! Besides, we need female Earthlings to do some special work in preparation for the great awakening of You-Know-Who! If I were you, I would head back to that tiny lonely island of yours until we call you back."

"I believe nothing you have to say, and I don't owe you anything! I'm a free man, I'm not a Prince now. A magician, a friend to animals and people, even those that are powerless. That's who I am. You can return and tell that to my father and everyone back at home!" I retort, wrestling to keep my sentences straight in the frosty weather. My limbs are shaking, but I won't back down.

"How dare you?" The man snaps, his feet taking an unwelcome step forth. His eyes glow with wrath.

The elf perseveres with its music – calm, composed, clear and compelling. Compelling enough to help a furious man bridle his fury.

Blowing out a few restless breaths, he then pulls from his coat a golden flute. He poses it in the valley of his palms and presents it to me with the grace of an official courtier.

Though hesitant at first, I accept it. Come to think of it, I needed a new flute. "Your father has sent me to hand this over to you. He wants all the family to be ready when the time comes."

"Time for what...?"

"Time is up," the man concludes, looking around as if expecting someone to suddenly appear.

The elf's song quivers ever so slightly, and I observe the shapes of its notes morph. The hair on my neck is stiff, my instincts alert.

"If those Earthling peasants even dare touch you or arrest you – Azwan's lion dragons are ready to come to your aid!" The man warns.

I want to press him, eager to know what he's referring to, but before I can, a dust of cloud is born, out of nowhere. Clearly, I'm not the only magic user here!

"Remember the missing children. They could be your doom...or your salvation!"

"What?" My heart leaps, pounding against my ribcage. What can he possibly know about the missing children? However, before I can open my mouth, he disappears in the cloud of white smoke, leaving behind an echo of his horribly deep laugh.

And with him vanishes the elf like a wisp in the wind. But not before the brush of its magical tunes against the ears of my animal friends, erases all memory they have of this encounter.

***

I'm left there standing in the snow with no further answers but holding this exquisite flute. I inspect it. It has an engraving of a lion with two wings. It's ironic that the engraving has wings, which signal freedom, when I feel trapped. Trapped by destiny and the circumstances I'm in. I make the cloud disappear, and the animals come rushing to my side.

"Where have you been? You suddenly left us all alone in the carriage! You made us worry! We thought you went back to London or worse yet, Guernsey!" cried Chuka.

"Nothing happened! I'm all right," I assure him -and the others- as I feel all their eyes on me. I hate to lie, but they aren't ready to know the full truth about my origins. They say nothing else, but the glinting, intelligent look in their eyes makes me wonder when they'll bring it up again.

I look up, finding the towering trees fade before my eyes. We're left on a vast, snowy hill, where I can see the candlelit windows of houses below us in the distance. It's Hamelin. I get back in the chariot.

"Well, that was an adventure all right," Storm comments, shaking the snowflakes off her back. "I'm still alive, right?"

Storm gives her a gentle nudge with his antlers.

"Hey, you!" she protests.

"Yup, you're alive," he affirms.

I still find myself captivated by the glisten of the golden flute in the dark. I carefully store it away in my pouch.

"I hope you don't abandon us again when we get to Hamelin," Chuka says, finally relaxing his grip on my head as we continue our journey.

"You never know," I reply. "I'm still befuddled by it all."

I pull the reins gently, slowing the unicorns.

"What's up?" Storm squeaks. "I can't tell if you're trying to break or just don't know what you're doing."

It occurs to me that Chuka has a point. I can't go into Hamelin with all these valuables – or rather, things that could mean life or death for us. Even my golden flute! With its shiny recent appearance, they might think it's worth a lot of coins. What if I lose them? What if the townspeople strip me of everything I own before beheading me, and my poor pets can't return to the refuge of Guernsey ever again? But I am not leaving them behind either – ever since the encounter I have no reason to trust this place.

I hear Storm moan in fear. "Or go back to London," she sighs.

"Maybe you will leave us for another adventure."

"Would you do that to us?" Chuka asks.

I am at a loss for words. Would I ever abandon my animal friends? I love them with all my heart – they are my dearest friends. All I can do is pat Chuka's head and invite poor Storm into a warm hug.

We head down the hill, reaching a plateau where we come across an abandoned burrow that's coated in snow. I jump out of the chariot and feel a rustling in one of my pockets. I quickly slide my hand inside and find a fuzzy creature. It's Fatso. I wonder if he heard everything between me and the music elf? Or he too was made to forget the whole encounter? I pull him out to make sure he's okay. I'd almost forgotten about him being with us! He looks up at me with his shiny black eyes, wiggling his pink nose and clasping a piece of carrot he's delectably nibbling.

He looks content but immediately shivers. I put him back in the tiny wool enclave of my pocket.

"Hang tight, little guy," I tell him, petting his furry back. "We're almost there."

I approach the burrow and drop the golden flute inside the pouch. I'm about to bury it alongside with Spinky' s jewels in the royal blue velvet drawstring bag under the snow when I hear the whistling of the wind. The sound seems to tell me something – or maybe it's just a musician's ear! The ground rumbles and I almost lose my balance! The unicorns topple like dominoes over each other, crying out in shock. We're all completely spooked.

"Last time you do that," Chuka comments, hanging on tightly to my neck for dear life. I resort to monitoring the flute closely and leaving it in my pocket. They all nod, but I can tell they're disturbed by the thought.

We continue to head down the hill, towards the clusters of houses. It's not the buzzing Hamelin that I remember. Could it be that it's already dusk, or because it's winter? It's difficult to gather our bearings in the falling snow, but I spot a building whose windows glow in a motley array of colours. Its stained glass. As we near it to take advantage of the light, I tug the reins. My heart jumps. Studying the picture, it's a man in a hat and tunic playing a flute, with a fan base of the children behind him. It's me! The Pied Piper! Should I feel honoured or afraid? I take a deep breath, and we continue onwards towards the main square.

We pass through a park with a frozen-over pond in the middle. Above it, a massive statue stands, coated in the white of snow. I don't think twice about it, but maybe it's just because I don't want to.

"Look at that!" Chuka cries.

"It's you!" Storm affirms.

"Me?" I try not to believe them.

But I know they're right.

The statue portrays a barefoot man holding a flute to his lips, followed by rows of entranced children who seem to glide over the water! My eyes shine in a hideous red colour and my mouth is quirked in a twisted imitation of my usually warm smile. I look downright scary in that statue. It reminds me of the bronze statue in London – was it some kind of prophecy I wonder? They're making me seem a criminal for their own purposes of pinning everything on me.

"What can I say?" I reply, trying to stay calm. "I'm famous here."

I take a deep breath again, reminding myself of my mission, imagining my lovely wife waiting for me - waiting to take me into her arms and tell me all of this has been worth the gruelling journey. I sincerely hope that Sherbert and Pepe are not as talented in lying as I'd been in London.

Just when I've regained my hope and faith, we reach the town square. Not a single person is even traversing in the blizzard. I pull the reins to park in the corner, so we can decide on our next course of action. As I pull myself out of the chariot, I catch sight of a poster plastered on the wall. It wouldn't have concerned me; except I could make out the word "Wanted" at the top. With my bare, nearly frostbitten hand, I sweep off the snow covering the rest. On it is the silhouette of a head playing a flute, and below it reads, "The Pied Piper – wanted for child theft. Dead or alive. Reward: 1,000 gold coins." Suddenly, a thought springs to my mind. I know who let my people know my plans. It was Pepe and Sherbert! I realise that Sherbert and Pepe, with their Skraa pap pap, was a clue to where they had been. I sigh. It will be an interminable day.

CHAPTER 7

THE PRINCE OF SHEBA

I had already planned that no matter what happened that day, I would see to it that I'd sleep at Snowphia's house. I wanted to see her up close. I wanted to see her for myself, to know her personality, her dreams, and her spirit. I wasn't sure whether I could trust a couple of ravens to make the right decision for me.

We arrive at much fanfare. Everywhere we go; young and old have their hearts set on having a look at the Prince of Sheba. It's inspiring that the children take a liking to us, otherwise seeing that statue in the Hamelin park would have broken my spirit. Everywhere I turn, there's some awful reminder of my last visit here. For a moment, it flashes through my mind what kind of horror would erupt if the town found out I was the very man who has taken away their children away. But perhaps time is a healer.

I continue walking through the crowd in my elegant suit and strutting with confidence to the front of the sad looking streets. "Is that a real Prince?" I hear kids whispering to each other.

"Come over here, little fellow," I say, waving one of the boys over. If only he knew how much of a show I must put on to pull off this scheme.

"Now, I want you to make a wish - but do not tell me what it is," I tell him. His eyes beam with immediate enthusiasm. "After you make your wish, I'm going to pull something out of this bag, and you'll see it's exactly what you wished for!"

"Really?" he exclaims, clapping his hands in joy.

"Are you ready?"

He bobs his head as an indisputable yes.

"Tres, Dos, Ein." I count down and then pull out one of the toys I bought in Hamley's, it's one of the archery sets. The boy widens his eyes in surprise.

"How did you know?" he shouts, examining his new bow and arrow to see if they are real. I give him a pat on his back, as people respond with a round of applause. I have managed to pull the wool over their eyes. This is a town which is ravaged by poverty, so anything I take out of the bag is going to be more than welcome by any child. I've taken my chances and I'm pulling it off!

Now I must try to find my way to Snowphia's house. For my next trick, I must make it look like I've been recommended to her family - the Blumenthals. I motion for everyone to pause their commotion.

"Erm, I have here a letter for Mr. and Mrs. Blumenthal. It is from my superiors back home in the Royal Palace of Sheba. Can anyone direct me to their house?"

A sea of jealous faces stares back at me. Apparently, each one of them wishes it were their house that would host this mystery Prince with milk and cookies that evening. But little do they know that this Prince is on a love mission! Or, perhaps, it's them who they think will get food. That would explain the ruckus surrounding me as I move. I can see myself through the eyes of the townspeople: not only am I overflowing with riches, I'm also going around with animals as company, so I must have food with me!

"Anyone?" I yelp.

"Well, they live down there," one of the boys speaks up, pointing down the side street. I look in that direction, and lo and behold, it's exactly as Sherbert and Pepe described – a house with a crumbling brown roof and cracked blue shutters, some of which are falling off the windows. It looks more like a rundown inn than anything else. Perhaps the man I'd met in the forest wasn't lying after all. That house - if it is the right one - screams poverty from the outside. I just hope the company of Snowphia will help me feel at home.

I'm slightly nervous as I walk up to the steps. There's a squeak from the pocket of my coat. I pull it open, finding Fatso contentedly chewing on a piece of carrot. His calmness soothes me. Once I gather enough courage, I knock on the front door. No one comes to the door.

"If they are not home, you can always stay at my house!" shouts one of the women from behind me. I hear the crowd grow louder as they whisper and gossip about what's going on. Suddenly, the door opens and before me stands a noticeably short man.

"You must be Mr. Blumenthal?" I ask confidently. "I'm the Prince of Sheba, from the Nubian Kingdom here to bear gifts for the children this Christmas. I apologize if I'm asking too much of you but the townspeople told me the Blumenthals are the family to ask for a place to rest my head."

He squints in confusion. It doesn't surprise me. I'm just better at hiding the overflow of emotions swimming through my head.

"Sir, any news of kindness and generosity tends to reach Lapland faster than a hungry eagle."

"Perhaps I shall let you in."

All I must do is bet that no human being will deny open arms to a stranger in need.

And that no one will notice the striking resemblance between my –admittedly exaggerated- portraits and statue. So far, so good. Nothing seems out of the ordinary, at least, to my standards. In no time I'll be able to see the marvellous Snowphia for myself. I hope I'm not making any incorrect assumptions about her.

Ever since first hearing about her, something inside me calls to be by her side. I know that she's beautiful, but secretly, I hope that she's also intelligent and sweet. I want her to be my beacon of hope and I don't know if that's asking too much. Reaching for a dream, a cloud of smoke that I won't ever get to see in person. I wish I could ask her outright once I meet her, but even I know that that's too extreme.

Mr. Blumenthal closes the door behind me, and I hear the crowd dispersing.

"Why can't they wait until Christmas for their gifts?" I ask, just to fill the awkward silence. It makes me look the part.

"It has been a while since this town has had something good happen to it," Mr. Blumenthal answers as he hands me a tin cup with what I believe is tea.

It turns out to be warm water with some sugar in it. I want to spit it out. Any hotter and I would have thought it's a napalm attack. I've heard that prisons would torture their inmates by applying sugar and boiling water to the skin, causing the flesh to melt. Alas, maybe this was some insidious form of punishment the town has planned for me!

"Thank you, sir," I simply say as I take another painful sip. Snowphia better be worth it! There's a knock at the door. It even spooks Fatso who has thus far remained ever so quiet in my big pockets. I lightly pat him to calm his fright.

"Ah, it must be my daughter back from prison!" he shouts as he walks down the hallway towards the door.

Wait…prison? She'd just been released from prison? Beautiful she'll be, perhaps. Generous to animals, a possibility. But what on earth has she done to get thrown in prison? I look around the room and the irony of it all snaps me out of my silly reverie. I'm a wanted criminal falling hopelessly in love with a woman I haven't actually met…that's also been charged as a criminal. My life is ridiculous. And I'm too trusting; she could be a thief for all I know! What do Sherbert and Pepe know about love anyway? All they seem to do properly is sing and gossip, and look where that's led me: back in Hamelin where everyone's after my blood.

I bite my cheek to keep myself from sighing and look stoically at my trembling hands, holding the cup. Then again, this is the "child thief" himself speaking. Do I have the right to question her motives? When I look up from my cup, there she is, standing in the hallway.

I lose my breath.

She's more than worth it. Comparing her to a million stars in the firmament and the most beautiful flowers in the world would not do her justice. She has an unprecedented beauty with her ocean-blue eyes and natural-looking hair.

Her father is speaking but I can't hear him – it's just noise in the background. I know it's rude of me to ignore the man, but I can't help it. I'm entranced by her beauty. I have never seen angels before, but I'm sure she is one of them. Is it those big, inquisitive eyes? Or that smile that radiates such purity of heart, such goodness – one which comes from deep within? Is it the way her honey-coloured curls peak out from under her scarf, or the way she places down her basket on the table with the grace of some ethereal being? Whatever it is, I fumble for the cup as it almost slips from my fingertips. Her beauty is remarkable.

I can only imagine what she thinks of me, though, in that white beard and puffy red suit. I doubt a prince was ever a candidate for the husband of her dreams.

"Hello sir, nice to meet you!" she greets cordially.

I'm speechless.

"Sorry. Erm," I swallow and clear my throat. "I thought your father implied you had been released from prison and I was trying to figure out what on earth a marvellous person like yourself had done to deserve that. I mean, if you were there, I wouldn't mind going to prison myself."

I could almost kick myself. All that royal training has gone to waste! I see the woman of my dreams, and all I can manage to speak about is how I have just finished theorizing her involvement with crime. Absurdly, I think that it's a good thing this is Hamelin and not London. Londoners are particularly stiff with their manners and a lady of society wouldn't allow this kind of behaviour if I were to court her.

She laughs out loud. Her voice has a clear-like sound, it has a harmonic ring that could simultaneously awake the storm within me and lull me to beautiful dreams. Viewing me as just a jolly old man with a sense of humour, Mr. Blumenthal breaks into a hearty laugh too.

"No sir, I help out at the prison," she corrects, blushing.

"What they say about this family is true," I remark.

"What might that be, sir?" she inquires.

"That you're loyal and valuable and anyone that meets you is lucky," I say slowly, looking at her. Because all I'm thinking of at the moment, is her. Her incandescent smile and clear eyes and the promises held in her sumptuous lips.

"I did not think Azwan was a real place," she replies.

"It is a real place; I can assure you." I give her a wink.

"Should I offer you something to eat?"

"You are far too kind. I will have whatever you give me." Anything other than warm sweet water is going to be a King's meal in my eyes.

I sit with Mr. Blumenthal at the kitchen table, as Snowphia heats up a lentil soup that she'd prepared the other day. But then, another smell fills —or should I say, attacks- my senses. The stench of fish enters my nostrils. I try hard not to scrunch up my nose. I don't want them to notice how repulsed by the smell I am, but I can't bear the thought of eating the fish! This could be one of my friends after all! How could I eat a friend of mine? That would be the act of a brute. My thoughts are spiralling out of control, and I ground myself to the present by looking at her. She's looking at me with uncertainty.

"Might I lend you a hand?" I ask, subconsciously wishing to impress her with my culinary skills, but signalling to the lentil soup. There's no way I'm helping with the fish, but it's already cooked anyway.

"Oh, no, sir," she says. "It's no work at all. We'll just leave it over the flame for a while and it will be ready in no time."

Don't call me sir, I want to say to her but instead, I nod curtly. Her father, on the other hand, desperately wants to engage me in a conversation about me being a Prince. He has heard about the queen of Sheba, my mother supposedly. I'm proud of making a good impression on him, he's going to be giving us his blessing in no time. I'm sure of that. I sit straight and regard him with a serious look.

"Oh, yes, yes, of course." I calm myself down, realizing I sound more thrilled by the prospect than I should. "We do get married. As for me, I have the misfortune of not yet finding the right woman. You see, I'm so famous that I suppose the women are …daunted. But how I would love to find a humble and kind woman to be by my side… I suppose from a land far away from my own." Snowphia turns to me, seemingly detecting what I am getting at.

"Well, my friend would be dearly pleased to know that you are looking for a betrothed here in Hamelin; after all, there's not much we can offer now, after the mess we have for home," Mr. Blumenthal replies with pursed lips.

I can't miss the opportunity to investigate the current situation of my future family. After all, being in disguise makes me even more courageous than I would be otherwise. "But sir, not to be rude, but why ask for a friend when your own lovely daughter is here?"

Silence pervades the kitchen. I wince, realizing that I might have overstepped my place. I hope they won't be throwing me outside to the street.

"Oh, sorry," I yelp, smacking my hand against my forehead. Stupid me! Now I've made myself look insensitive and impertinent to both of them.

"Have you noticed that you haven't met Snowphia's mum yet?" Mr. Blumenthal asks dryly. "Have you wondered why?"

Of course, I should have thought of it before speaking. The fact that there's only this man and his daughter is strange. Most families here are big, having many siblings besides the mother and father. I tilt my head downwards briefly and raise it again to explain my behaviour.

"Well, I hadn't thought about it." My face tenses. I wish the ground would devour me and I could disappear then and there. "Forgive me if I offended you."

"You see, she has been bedridden for years. She was possessed by demons after losing our daughter to the Pied Piper. You don't have to feel bad. The day we allowed that cursed Piper in our town was the day all this madness started! Sometimes I wish I could see him and eliminate him with my bare hands. How is it okay for him to have walked out of this place without any consequences while we're all starving, dirt poor and have torn families? My wife and I built a future for our daughters and what do we have left? What do I have left, good sir?" he exclaims, slamming his fist against the table.

I look at him perplexed.

"I'll tell you what I have, good sir. I have a bedridden wife, an overworked daughter, and a pile of bills! Two rations a day can't fill anyone-"

Snowphia intervenes.

"That's quite enough father. You must be terrifying His Highness."

"You know it's not good for your health to get like this - look at mother. She's suffering because she can't get a hold on her anger and pain. I don't want you to suffer like that," she says, slowing rubbing circles on his back.

My heart jumps. I swallow. I feel my hands start to shake slightly, and I wonder if they're ever going to be able to forgive me once they inevitably find out. The man deflates on his seat, and with that act, the tension dissipates in the room. I can almost feel the air around the room changing as he sits, chastened and calm.

"Forgive me for the outburst, Your Highness. We've gone through a lot. Snowphia is always here by my side."

"Ah, the Pied Piper?" My voice cracks. "I'm sorry to hear that."

"Maddie, my beautiful daughter. You should have seen her. And on that fateful day, I lost not one but two important women in my life. Maddie and my wife." He frowns, holding in his tears.

"Every day we have to tell Mama that Maddie is coming back," Snowphia clarifies, twisting her neck towards me while stirring the cauldron of the soup. "It's the only way to keep her happy. Though we're sure my poor sister is alive no more."

I grow increasingly uneasy, ashamed that I've been invited into the house of a family whose lives I've unwillingly shattered. I don't know whether to stay silent and mask this guilt under my disguise or reveal my true identity and beg for their forgiveness. Either way, any hope of being with Snowphia is gradually draining. So be it, I'll get my due punishment: being alone forever, just like Sherbert joked I would.

"Snowphia is the only child we have left. We cannot let her go."

Those words are the final stab to my heart. I had the feeling he'd say something like this after his outburst, but still, I was hoping he wouldn't insist on her staying, after seeing my immense wealth and that I could provide them with a better life. It seems like I'm always hoping.

I take a deep breath. But what good does self-pity serve? Wasn't it me who chose to never stop believing in the generosity of a stranger? The town is in shambles. All they have is me now. I can't let them down, and I can't let the Blumenthals down. Not after all the suffering they've been through – all because of my past foolishness.

My thoughts are interrupted by Snowphia's sweet voice. "Kind sir, would you like some bread with your soup?" I gaze at her striking blue eyes that radiate such innocence, not having a clue who I really am. I can feel tears welling up in the ducts of my eyes. To think, she'll never enjoy the beauty of romantic love – with me or anybody - because of what I have done.

Then she hums thoughtfully and –after deliberating something- she exclaims: "Oh! And we also have fish! It's the last we have and it's very good. Would you like some?" Her eyes are ponds where I could drown, I almost nod along distractedly. But refrain from doing it. Even pretending to eat the fish and making it disappear seems like a disservice to my pet companions. I can't do that, not even for her. So, I respectfully decline the fish and accept the lentil soup claiming that I ate enough at the Royal Palace (almost slipping a "we" in the process).

I eat the bread and soup in silence. It tastes delicious; I think they use a different recipe here.

"It is lovely," I praise.

She smiles warmly and reaches for my bowl after I finish the last spoonful. I can't help but extend my hand to hers.

"I'm so sorry," I murmur. She seems surprised at the genuine remorse in my eyes. Something in her eyes shift, but I can't think of how to properly describe it. Something changes once she realizes I'm truly sorry. I can't say if it's trust or something more special.

Will she come to see me the way I see her? Is it fate that I should be in this house? Have the ravens sent me to teach me a lesson?

"Just so you know, I will pay you for each night I spend here until Christmas," I assure Mr. Blumenthal. I want to give them everything I have brought with me.

"You do not have to, sir. Your company is enough."

"No, I insist. You can use the money to get a nurse for your wife. And you can buy enough food to eat well. It's the least I can do."

"Thank you," Mr. Blumenthal replies. "I never imagined we'd meet a distinguished member of the Royal Family. A Prince! Imagine if your mother could understand this, Snowphia," he says gleefully. "The honour is ours. But it's no surprise to me that he's one of the most generous and gracious men I've encountered in my life."

Snowphia and I exchange a look and the briefest of smiles forms on her cherry-red lips. It disappears quickly but it's quite an enticing look that I don't suppose I'll ever be able to forget.

He turns to his daughter. "Snowphia?"

"Yes, Papa?" she says, reluctantly flicking her eyes to his.

"Please prepare the bed for our guest." He looks at me and adds, "I'm afraid we don't have much – we can only afford so much firewood, but the warmest room is yours."

"You don't have to -"

"I insist," he interrupts me.

I follow Snowphia, who tucks clean linens into the bed, and throws on top three thick blankets. She hands me a stack of clothing.

"Here's some pyjamas for you. I'll prepare some hay for your unicorn horse, and your pet monkey can have the rest of the soup," she adds with a small smile. Right then and there, I yearn to marry her. That I know. Yes, I've lied about news of their kindness reaching Lapland. It has reached much further than that. It has reached me in Guernsey, an island beyond this world. But my greatest hope has sunken to the worst punishment I can imagine. I can never marry the one and only woman I know I can truly love.

Or can I? For a long time, I have been convinced that Hamelin is wrong. Indeed, perhaps the Mayor is wrong, but who cares now?

The young woman before me flashes another smile and approaches the doorway to respectfully leave me alone.

"Snowphia," I say.

She stops and turns around.

"Please take this pearl necklace and earrings, it's a simple gift that pales compared with a beautiful lady such as you," I say, throwing her a bashful glance. I place them in the palm of her hand, and they glisten next to the candlelight.

"Oh, mama would love these!" she remarks.

"This is for you."

"W-what?" Her lips part and her ocean eyes open wide in wonder. Her lips – which have an exquisite rosy colour that could awake emotions in the coldest men- and her creamy hands tremble as she takes it.

"A gift for you," I insist, resisting the urge to ask her if I can kiss her hand and play my music to her under the starry sky.

I lay my head on the pillow, with Snowphia's bright eyes being my only comfort as I attempt to fall asleep. I think of her joy at my small gift – I yearn to give her a million more for many years to come. I don't think she's going to appreciate me being here for too long. I hope the gift changes her impression of me. She seemed different earlier. Perhaps I overwhelmed her, but now she looks calm.

Everything about her. I like everything about her. I hope she'll come to see me as the only one for her. I wonder what she looks like wearing the necklace. What she thinks of me. I just want to tear this disguise off my face and touch the soft skin of her face. And I can only imagine the horror on her face when she discovers I'm the child thief. The one who robbed her and her family of her beloved sister.

I feel a knot of pain in my stomach. What do I have to do to make them forgive me? To make the town forgive me? To make them see it's the money-hungry Mayor who robbed a poor piper of his modest pay and that I didn't know what else to do?

I take a deep breath and decide I'll deal with reality tomorrow. As I shut my eyes, I remember that Fatso is still in the pocket of my coat. I've forgotten to feed him tonight! I jump up from the bed.

The pocket is empty. Oh no, this isn't the time for this to happen - I hear a scream.

***

Fatso wiggles his tiny pink nose, searching the floor for any crumb he can find. Before he knows it, his nose has hit right into the wall of the hallway. It's pitch black inside the house now that everyone has gone to sleep. He shuffles his little paws across the floor, scurrying into what he's quite sure is the kitchen. Fatso runs into a pillar of wood. Aha! The kitchen table.

He crawls up the leg of the table and grabs onto the tablecloth. Sniffing around, he smells something delicious. Is it blueberry pie? Cinnamon muffins? Cherry Tarts? He can't tell. Fatso runs over to it, his mouth watering, and begins chewing the sweet dessert with his tiny sharp teeth.

Ahhhhhhhhhhhhhhhhhhh! A shriek sounds. He's thrown against the wall when the food sits up. And so, he realizes it's not food. It's Snowphia. He'd been chewing her hair. But she smells wonderful, like fruit and cereals and it's been so long since he last ate! Oh, but how can he explain this to his friend?

Mr. Blumenthal runs into the room and lights a candle at once, convinced his daughter is being abducted or killed. It wouldn't be so unlikely, after all the problems they've been going through.

I'm searching for Fatso all around my room when I hear the scream. I'm already gathering that he's gotten out and crossed paths with my beloved. I run through the hallway, finding Snowphia's door open and a candle lit inside.

"A rat! A rat!" she's screaming. "A rat was eating my hair!"

Mr. Blumenthal hears a squeak from below and lowers the candle, finding Fatso frozen in fear. Suddenly, Fatso sprints out of the bedroom and zooms down the hallway. Mr. Blumenthal runs after the critter. I light a lantern and follow him. Just when he seems to have cornered Fatso at the front door, my pet rat squeezes out of the crack under the door into the freezing winter's night.

Oh, no. This is a worse disaster than I could imagine.

"A rat! A rat!" Mr. Blumenthal yells, after tearing open the door and chasing Fatso down the street. "Get the police! There's a rat in Hamelin!"

One by one, I see the windows of houses illuminate. A neighbour opens the door, still in her nightgown. "A rat? Where?"

Woken in the middle of the night, the neighbours gather outside with their lanterns and candles, driven to even more commotion than they had been when Santa visited.

"Who brought a rat to Hamelin?" I hear one neighbour ask.

"It must be that mysterious man!" a woman accuses. "He brought a rat from his nation! It must be a complot to make us go insane!"

"There's no rats where I come from!" someone protests.

"I'd say there are!" another neighbour chimes in.

Everyone mumbles in agreement. I can almost sense them going after me and Fatso with torches.

Oh no.

Didn't I already say that?

Double oh no.

"Did they find it?" I hear Snowphia ask quietly behind me, as I stand at the open doorway. Suddenly, there's a realization that I've gotten myself into something bigger than what I expected. I turn to her, and she looks at me with a small wrinkle forming between her eyebrows. Her clear, innocent, eyes give me a sharp look and then they change to something strong. I see accusation and mistrust in them.

"Who are you? Are you a Prince or not?"

My lips open and close slowly and I wonder what I can do before speaking to her. She comes slightly closer to me than what should be considered proper.

"You can tell me, but once this is over, I want to know what's going on," the way she looks at me is somewhere in-between mistrust and interest. Of course, she'd find me interesting when I've gotten myself into this issue! On the plus side, by the glisten in her eyes, she seems to find me more handsome than she'd previously deemed. I step out of the doorway and run down the street, determined to rescue Fatso before anyone else gets to him. As I slip into a dark corner, I'm distracted by the piercing scream of a woman from somewhere behind me.

"The rat! The rat! The rats are back! I told my husband that the town was cursed, and he wouldn't believe me!" The woman seems deeply anguished; it sounds like she has lost her mind.

I hold my breath and throw myself against a wall, desperately keen to avoid detection. I quickly scan the streets for Fatso, assuming he must be somewhere nearby. I reach into my pocket to make sure I've brought my flute just in case a charm session is necessary to get this little fellow out safely. Within a few seconds, Hamelin's own secret police, the Gustavo arrive on the scene.

"Now, now then, what's all this kerfuffle about? Good men and women should be in their beds at this hour, nothing good can come of being in the streets."

"You're right that nothing good is afoot - look!" shrieks the woman once more. "It's a blooming rat! And I saw lots more at the same time - the rest of them scarpered when they realized I was after them! We have to warn the Mayor, and every citizen of Hamelin - surely it means that he'll be coming back!"

I don't think she's going after me, but I still feel attacked.

"Calm down there, missus," the Gustavo sighs. "We haven't seen a rat in these parts for quite some time, and we're not about to start now. That's not even a rat anyway. It's just a harmless little mouse, see? Just a harmless, fat little mouse."

The Gustavo removes his truncheon from his belt and approaches the creature in question. I'm about to run towards them from my hiding place, in fear that they're going to injure my poor little Fatso, but I hesitate. If I do, we'll both be dead, that's for sure!

"Come 'ere, little one. Can't have you upsetting the ladies of the town now, it's just not on. One whack and it'll all be over, and we'll roast you up for supper!"

Fatso catches sight of me with frightened eyes. Before I can make a move, down goes the stick, with the crack of wood on pavement echoing throughout the streets, missing Fatso by several inches.

"Damn and blast! I knew I shouldn't have drunk that bottle of port before I went on duty this evening!" the Gustavo grumbles. "And now there are two of them!"

"Oh, for goodness sake you're a drunken buffoon, give me that," the woman snaps, snatching the stick from Gustavo's hands. "I'll deal with this."

Seeing her swing the weapon toward Fatso, I can't take it anymore. "No! Leave him alone!" I cry, emerging from the shadows and scooping the little mouse up in my hands. In exchange, I earn a crack in the back of my knuckles from the truncheon and almost drop Fatso.

"Now, what's all this then?" the Gustavo asks me. "Who are you, and why are you so concerned about a mouse? And why on earth are you wearing a pair of lady's bloomers, are you in some kind of disguise?"

"That doesn't matter," I stammer. "I am just a humble traveller with a love for all creatures. I come to your town seeking worms."

"Worms?" replies the Gustavo.

"Worms?" the woman echoes.

"Squeak," says Fatso.

"Worms," I concur. "I seek worms for food. I can see that there are no such things here, however, so I shall stop wasting your time and take my leave of you and your delightful little town. I'll take the mouse with me and make sure that he does not frighten any more of the local women."

Hopefully, they'll leave me in peace.

As the I rotate my heel and turn to depart, the Gustavo places a burly hand on my shoulder.

"Hold on, hold on. Not so fast. I have some questions for you, stranger."

"Oh?" I gulp.

"Yes. I don't like mysteries, and you're not being straight with me. I'll amend my line of questioning. I don't care why you're wearing lady's bloomers, but where did you get them from? I find them quite striking and, if they come in a bigger size, I'd like to get some for my wife."

"Oh, for goodness sake!" the woman cries. "Don't you see? He seeks worms for food - he has found a source of fish! We have to learn where this is - it's the only way that the town of Hamelin can survive."

"Hmm." The Gustavo strokes his chin thoughtfully. "That does make sense. OK then, let's be having you. Where are these fish of yours?

My throat runs dry as I desperately try to concoct an answer. There is no way I can explain the invisible ocean – they'll surely think me mad and send me to the asylum. On the other hand, if they somehow find a way to reach Guernsey, my friends will be hunted all over again.

"I'm sure that I recognize him, you know," the woman tells the Gustavo. "Ask him his name."

"Do not assume to tell an officer of the law his duty, madam!" the Gustavo indignantly replies. He turns to me, following up with, "now then, what's your name?"

"Wilhelm, "I say, using the first name that pops into my head. I don't even know if I've met any Wilhelms in my life, or why I think of it.

"This is Wilhelm," the Gustavo tells the woman. "Well, that's another mystery solved. On your way then, Wilhelm. I heard there was someone out and about looking for worms and I want to catch him, not waste my time gasbagging with you."

"That's him, you do it!" the woman cries. "Tell him to turn out his pockets, he's up to something, I'm sure of it."

"Right then sir, I feel that it is my duty as a police officer to ask you to turn out your pockets," the flatfoot says.

I freeze, debating whether to make a run for it. If I lose Fatso in the process, I'll have even more guilt on my plate. What am I protecting myself from anymore? I can never marry Snowphia. I've destroyed her family, after all. Maybe it is the time I face my guilt and allow destiny to take me where it should. The Gustavo snatches his truncheon from the woman and raises it towards me as a threat. Reluctantly, I comply with his orders. The moment my hand curls around the flute, I know that the jig is up.

"It's the Pied Piper!" I hear a man's voice shout from behind her. It's Mr. Blumenthal. Next, to him, Snowphia's shocked blue eyes are staring at the spectacle. "First, he takes my daughter! And now he's brought rats back to the town! He's a monster, I tell you!"

"I knew he'd return!" the woman howls. "Arrest him at once!"

A chorus of shouts and insults erupt throughout the crowd. My nightmare has come true. But nothing shatters my soul more than seeing Snowphia witness my humiliation. That, more than anything, is the true nightmare. She looks at me and she seems disappointed. This is the reason why I wasn't willing to risk myself at the beginning.

Solemnly, I raise my hands in defeat and let the Gustavo frog put his handcuffs around my arms, Fatso nervously staring at me and the officers. I have the distinct feeling that this is only beginning, and the worst is yet to come.

CHAPTER 8

THE RAT IS OUT OF THE BAG!

Sometimes life isn't kind to us. Sometimes you can't get what you want. I found that out once upon a time when I had to run from where I came from. But now, I'm still here wondering why I can't help but run into trouble every time I do something.

So, how did I get here? Well, once I came to stand in-between the raging people and Fatso, I made a motion that made my flute fall to the ground, causing people to realise who I was.

The one and only Pied Piper! Feared and hated by this town. Casted from his nation and runaway Prince. Now, I'm those things AND heartbroken by Snowphia's look of mistrust and judgment. I purse my lips and cast a questioning glance to Fatso. He looks at me before casting his head low. He seems ashamed.

Good. It's his fault for going after Snowphia's hair when he knows I could provide him food. Sometimes I wonder why my friends are so wild. Then I remember they are animals, after all. It still bothers me.

As I move with my jailers, I think of everything I've ever done. Is this a punishment for not being obedient? But what or who could punish someone for being kind to animals, who are innocent and pure unlike humans? Who would do that? And why?

Now I'm here sitting behind these bars and a few men enter the room, giving me dirty looks.

"SCUM!" screams one and the other one stops him.

"I don't want to lose any time, focus on our task," says the other man calmly.

They step outside and I sag against the dirty walls and even dirtier floor, where Fatso appears after running for quite a long time...

***

Outside, no one could understand how the Pied Piper managed to fool the townspeople again. A man was awoken by the ongoing sounds of the town screaming –and even crying- that could be heard outside every house.

"What time is it?" the man grumbled, holding a candle as he stood at his doorstep. "What is so important that it cannot wait until the morrow?"

He'd been having a wonderful dream where he was eating a giant-sized cake and drinking fruit juice until he felt nauseous and then a beautiful woman had come into the scene holding a fruit basket with a smile upon her face...

He shouldn't be awakened when he was having such a perfect dream.

"Sir, we have just been told to wake you up and let you know there is an emergency meeting at the town hall."

"Who else is going? That Fat Bastard better be there too. Let me get dressed and be on my way."

He swung the door closed and dragged himself back to his room, tucking himself into bed again.

"Pointless meetings," he muttered to himself. "I am not losing sleep over these stupid pointless meetings."

Another knock sounded at the door.

"Who is it?" he shouted, not bothering to get up this time. He heard a muffled response but couldn't make out what was being said.

"Leave me alone!" he shouted back. "Tell the mayor I am unwell, and I feel very sickly."

"Very well sir," the voice replied, "I guess you will not be involved in the Pied Piper's fate."

"The - what?"

A twisted smile formed on Captain Hook's lips. He thought retirement would be too boring, but his day was only getting better. Maybe it was even worth it to be awakened from his dreams if it meant he was getting to be involved in this. They walked towards the town hall. He was half-dressed, and still half-asleep.

"Did he bring the children back with him?" he asked a bit belatedly.

"Probably not, by the look of it," said the other man.

"So, what brings him back here?"

"Gentleman, have a seat," the Mayor instructed, again pulling out his handkerchief and dabbing off the drops of sweat from above his brow. "My sincere apologies for waking you up so late in the night like this. But Christmas has come early."

***

Many of the councilmen still had their nightgowns on, frowning at having been awaken in the middle of the night for an impromptu meeting.

"Shush!" Mr. Blumenthal hissed, trying to help keep the meeting on track. The young scribe next to the Mayor dipped his feather pen in the inkwell.

"So, gentlemen," the Mayor began. "The Pied Piper thought it clever of him to strike again. But as I have always told you, we should be prepared for the worst – and I have always been proven right."

He chuckled to himself.

"See, gentleman? I'd predicted it!"

He scanned his captive audience, making sure they comprehended what he was getting at.

"The reason why you are all here is to decide how best to rid of the Pied Piper once and for all. The world will look to us, gentlemen, to mete out justice, and we should do it in a way to make our message loud and clear."

The Mayor paused dramatically. The room erupted into screams.

"I say we hang him!"

"I say we burn him in a bonfire for Christmas!" one of the council members interjected.

"Yes!"

"Hang him!"

"Burn him!"

The members of the council jeered. Mr. Blumenthal, on the other hand, sat in silence. The last thing he wanted his neighbour to know was that he'd just dined with the Pied Piper.

"Order, order!" the Mayor shouted, striking his gavel on the wooden table. "I say we cut his head and burn him in the bonfire!" another man exclaimed, ignoring the Mayor.

The jeers became even louder. The room was full of energy as if it were a celebration.

"Alright, alright. I like the idea of cut and burn," the Mayor agreed. "I'm sure we can arrange for the bonfire. But as for the beheading…"

The grey-haired Captain Hook stood up. "Sir, with all respect, I have served this town for many years now and I beg that you give me the honour to retire with grace and have the pleasure to be the man with the hand that nails the Piper."

The men cheered in support of the idea.

"I would give you the honour," the Mayor replied. "But can you handle the Diele?"

"I can use the guillotine with one hand. I have one mighty arm on me, sir -"

"This is a German event, and we will use German equipment," the Mayor interrupted.

"Humph," Captain Hook muttered under his breath, slumping back down in his seat.

"Everything German. We do not want the French to take credit. Then they'll end up selling more of their guillotines to the world. The Diele is marvellous, spectacular. More impressive to the eye than even the circus or theatre! There's so much more to an execution than just dropping the blade and ending the show early."

The Mayor broke into a sinister laugh. The councilmen chuckled as well – all except for Mr. Blumenthal, who was less than pleased with the direction the meeting was going.

"I want the event to be… legendary!" the Mayor exclaimed. The councilmen roared and clapped in agreement.

"Hamelin's greatest execution of all time," Lez murmured to himself, taking note of his next headline.

"Sir?" Mr. Blumenthal raised a shaky hand.

The Mayor couldn't even hear him with the noise in the room.

"Sir!" Mr. Blumenthal raised his voice, standing up.

Finally, the Mayor came back to his senses and struck the gavel on the table three times.

"Order!" The loud voices faded to only hushes.

"You speak of your fancy plans to behead this man, but what about the children? Might you first interrogate the Pied Piper to find out what he has done with them? To see whether they are still alive?"

"What about the Christmas gifts he brought?" another council member sarcastically chimed in.

"Ask him for those as well!"

The room filled with shouts and applause again. Lez raised his hand and stood up.

"Truly, Mayor, what about the children?"

"I second that!" Mr. Blumenthal concurred. "Nearly every family has lost a child, and a wealth of gifts are not going to dry our tears right now. I say we interrogate the Pied Piper and find out where he's taken our sons and daughters."

There was a pause in the room and the councilmen looked at each other. It's as if they didn't care to think for themselves and were waiting to see how the rest of their cronies would react.

"Can we auction off his flute when his head is in the bonfire?" one of them finally shouted with a twisted grin.

The men guffawed at the proposal. The Mayor finally called the meeting to an end. Mr. Blumenthal and Captain Hook dragged themselves out of the town hall, unsatisfied.

"He's just a corrupt crook," Mr. Blumenthal concluded.

"Aye for that," Captain Hook agreed.

Then another man spoke.

"Stealing children isn't his only crime. He also stole our fish and I don't see any of you complaining about it!"

The other men looked at him.

"Sir, do you have any proof of that? We have to trial this man against all his crimes!" exclaimed a woman.

"Of course. I know all about this because he stole those fishes from me," he says matter-of-factly.

"I say we execute him now!" exclaimed Captain Hook, but the Mayor stopped him.

"This sir is right," he said, pointing at Mr. Blumenthal, "he must know where the children are, so we have no choice but to get the truth out of him first."

Everyone agreed and Lez, who'd been eavesdropping, scurried out the room, and, as he walked out the door, he found himself wondering why this man could possibly be back knowing that he would face execution here. Surely, if he was so evil, he wouldn't be going back to the place where he committed his crimes, right? But he'd never dare risk his job to say it aloud. He took his parchment and started scribbling away with his fast pen.

This was going to be an excellent story.

CHAPTER 9

IN THE LION'S DEN

I hear dogs howling to my left. Their cries are so deafening that, without being able to see them, I thought for a moment that they were a pack of wolves ready to devour me. They'd blindfolded me. I'd asked them why.

"You are about to enter hell and we wouldn't want you to see your torturers, would we, Mr. Pied Piper?"

I don't like not being able to see. Even if I'm about to encounter the worse torture of my life, being blindfolded just makes me feel helpless. As they drag me into the musty prison of the castle, the putrid scent of decay fills my nostrils. The stones are cold and even worse, the floor is slimy against my shivering, bare feet.

Crooks, a fellow inmate and a runaway slave from Britain, tells me the blindfold is to stop me from learning the ins and outs of the prison in case I plan on trying to escape. I figure it may also serve to prevent me from seeing just how bad the place is. I imagine skeletons hanging from the walls, and blood coating the chamber floors.

"Just to warn you, whatever is about to happen, just know that if it doesn't kill you, it'll make you stronger," Crooks advises me, his chains clanking as he speaks.

"In my many years here as your Captain, I have never had any prisoner escape these four walls," Captain Hook declares. "I am about to retire, and I plan on keeping my proud record - if you dare even think about escaping, Mr. Pied Piper, I will let all hell loose on you! And since I cannot guarantee that you won't THINK to escape, I have here my friend Charlie THE NUTTER. In the next moments you will know why he's earned that nickname."

The room I'm in has no windows and its walls and floor are stained. The inmates are placed close to each other, making it suffocating to be here and the rancid stench of the littered scraps of food around the cell and the dirty bodies are enough to make me vomit. I've done it once already, but hunger is starting to break me and if I keep giving in to the powerful reaction I have to the smells, I'll be throwing up more times than I'd like.

I've met many men here that I can't describe as particularly pleasing but some of them aren't actually bad people. For example, poor Charlie the Nutter, who's a reminder of how unfair the treatment to the people of Hamelin is. Charlie is a man with a vacant expression, who enjoys making bewildering comments and is forced by Captain Hook to act as his law enforcer. It's a very sad affair. I don't think the man can be accused of understanding his actions whilst Captain Hook instigates his errant behaviour. Sometimes he comes to us and starts to laugh awkwardly.

"I'm sorry you're here, it's unfair and unnecessary," I say looking at Crook's downcast face.

"If you don't like this," says a voice behind us, "imagine what a noose around your neck or losing your head would feel like. It's always an excellent incentive for other inmates. Some of the men that have met me wish they would be given the mercy of a quick death or being confined in prison. I'm not particularly keen on any of them," says Captain Hook sarcastically.

He loves to point out to us how long we'll be here for, and I'm too exhausted to fight him off. I know he has all the power now.

"I want you to think deeply about what you've done and how you've destroyed other people's lives with your actions," he says, and then spits my face.

If I had my flute on me, he wouldn't be able to use his mouth to do any spitting –or talking- anymore. I swallow and dry my face on my shoulder, where the hideous uniform is covering my skin.

They take off my blindfold, and I find myself in a dark dungeon. The emaciated prisoners chained to the walls around me look devoid of life. I look up and cower at the grizzly bear of a man in front of me – towering in height, with a thick black beard and hands that could break my neck with a single twist. He seems like a monster in the body of a human, so bloodthirsty that he himself has been chained down to restrain him.

Charlie gives me a menacing look and I know I'll be fortunate if I make it until the day of my execution. He snarls when he sets eyes on me like a wild animal having captured its prey. I felt the hollowness of an empty stomach and the disgust of thinking that so many people are going through pain. It'd been a long day. But, instead of giving in the impulse of voicing my tiredness, I sigh.

"I have happy news for us," he says icily. "It was rather late when you came here last night, although I'm sure you must have noticed we have a new addition to this establishment. You have a new companion here," he says pointing at me.

I set my jaw brazenly to meet his stare.

"Now gentlemen, our Mr. Pied Piper is new to the prison and therefore, this calls for an initiation."

The room falls silent. Everyone pulls themselves up in their chains to watch as if they've had no other form of entertainment for months, if not years.

"After his initiation, I am sure any thoughts of escaping will vanish. Today will be slightly special in that Charlie here, could have turned out different if his two younger brothers had not been taken away by the Pied Piper," Captain Hook adds.

"This is bad," I mumble to myself. I hadn't realised how big these families were!

A Gustavo enters holding a set of heavy, iron keys. He unlocks Charlie's chains. My body tenses, hoping the adrenaline will cushion the blows. He charges at me like a lion entering battle, menace burning in his eyes. I have entered Charlie's den and he's about to make me his meal.

First, he grabs my ear between his teeth, writhing and pulling. He's not just a nutter, this man, but he's a cannibal! I try to throw him off me, but he's ten times stronger I am. Wherever I look, there's no way out. He's simply too strong and without my magic, his brutish force can bring me down easily.

He looks at me only for an instant and then he launches a few blows to my head. I look to the Gustavo to stop the onslaught. My only saving grace is that Captain Hook won't let me die in prison, lest he ruins the Christmas spectacle. I fall to the floor, and the beast stomps on my face with his large, wet sandals. I can taste everything he's set foot on that day – and trust me, in that disgusting prison; they are all things I'd rather not taste!

If I felt any pity for the man, it was gone out the door at that moment. Next thing I know, I black out.

"Without his flute, he is an animal like the rest of you - LOOK AT HIM!" Captain Hook sneers.

I vomit blood, and as he parades me around the cells where every man takes out their anger on me, I feel grateful for the few that only kick me half-heartedly, but the rest are cruel: they spit on me, call me names and punch me until I'm a bleeding mess. I have many bruises and a large cut across my jaw that I doubt will ever heal properly. That is, if I ever set a foot outside this prison. So much that my vision starts blurring...

***

I'm laying here in bed, tolerating the scrutinizing looks of the people surrounding me. Last night, they didn't get the time to attack me to their heart's content. Now, I'm here, and I can face the visages of my would-be attackers, and I don't feel too calm by looking at them. After their initiation, I was left a mess and sent straight to sleep. I obeyed their instructions and meekly went to bed, limping slightly.

One of the men is speaking to another one in hushed tones, describing all the things he'd do if he was out of prison. He's small and looks almost frail but has a small smile stuck to his dried lips. The other one replies and they both laugh.

Crooks asks me what I'd do.

"What about you, Mr. Pied Piper?" he says dryly.

"I'd go to a special place, with a very special lady and have my last dance with her." I say, because I don't see myself running away from this place so easily.

No, I know if they do what their hearts demand, I won't be able to survive this. One of the inmates looks at me with a predatory stare. He smiles and shows me his sharp, yellow teeth gleefully. Another one has a dark gaze that considers me briefly without too much interest. He has a faraway look as a shadow clouds his green eyes; his staring is both disturbing and intriguing. I feel a kinship to him.

Captain Hook regards me with a twisted smile. He moves forward, his prominent nose strutted to the front as he regards the prisoners. A guard that's proudly standing behind him speaks as he looks at me with a grim expression:

"If I were you, I'd be quiet and go back to sleep. You don't want to cause a scene in here, do you? Enjoy your last days in prison. Soon, your head will be on a pike in the town square for everyone to see."

***

Once he leaves, we can speak our minds quite easily. Not everyone is a violent grunt. Some want to be free, just like I do. Crooks, for example, has a curious gaze that showcases his underlaying gentleness. I can't picture him doing anything horrible.

We're speaking about things we like, and I give out a few reluctant answers to the food I like the most. He seems outraged at me eating only vegetables and fruit and I correct him:

"I eat legumes too. They're quite tasty, you should try them, sir."

He laughs heartily, but the smile doesn't quite reach his eyes.

"Where did you learn to play the flute?" he asks curiously.

I frown and get up fast, but I can't see in the dark. There's no use trying to leave a guarded room and I can't cast any magic without my music.

I sit down. I can't see around me, but I can sense the quietness of a room where almost everyone has gone to sleep. I guess I can tell him a few truths, here and there.

"I learned it at Tiffin's School of Music. I went there when I was a young boy and met many people from all around the world."

"Is it the same school I heard about? The one with wizards and witches?"

There's no doubt in my mind what he's thinking.

"Is it the one with the wizard boy that has the scar?"

I chuckle. It's almost endearing.

"I'm not a wizard, I'm a music magician," I reply wistfully.

It turns out not everyone is asleep, and I hear the repulsive voice of Charlie the Nutter speaking:

"If I were a Wizard, you would not be stuck in here with us!"

I quickly change the subject.

"I used to go around the world, saving people. I would rescue entire towns and resorted to freeing animals. I could never kill them. I can't even bear the idea of eating animal meat!"

Crooks looks baffled.

"I would set them free to go wherever they wanted to be."

"You mean to tell me you didn't kill the rats?"

I shook my head with a light chuckle. "No, I love animals too much and can't be that cruel to them. They are my friends."

Charlie the Nutter laughs maniacally.

"Such a lying little twiddle twaddle!"

"Sir, let him continue," says Crooks. "What kind of animals did you free?"

"I have freed dragons, bats, flying snakes, three-headed lions, camels, and giraffes. I'm a friend to all creatures, scary creatures in secret places have come to my aid," I recall calmly.

"I have them all. I went to Bagdad once. I'm looking forward to going back there, it was beautiful. Asia minor too, I got Boris the Spider there as a gift. He was in this small egg, and golden egg encasing. I've also been to the land of the scorpions and spiders and lastly, I landed in Hamelin."

That last thought saddens me.

Our small conversation is ended by the abrupt entrance of a guard with a cube that he splashes onto us. After, we're all freezing, I remain quiet as Crooks reasons with Charlie the Nutter, who's threatening to kill us for this.

***

The next day, I wake up in the dungeon, unable to move my aching, bruised body. In the corner is a wooden bucket filled to the rim with yellow liquid, and above it on the stone wall are brown smudges. By the sickening odour it emits, I have little doubt about what it's used for.

"Don't try to move too much until one of the girls comes to clean you up," says the voice next to me. It's Crooks. Poor woman! To be charged with the task of taking care of brute men that could attempt to hurt them too. I don't wish that upon my worst enemy.

"I won't," I reply, grateful that at least I'm making a new friend despite the terrible situation.

"When the girl comes, her beauty alone will heal you from the inside," he adds.

There is only one beautiful woman in my eyes in the whole of Hamelin. And I made her angry. Someone as noble and honest as Snowphia won't be able to forgive me for lying to her and taking her sister away. I hope she'll be able to forgive me sometime in the future. I wish I could see her smile and her innocent –and calm- ocean eyes...

Wait a minute.

Isn't Snowphia the girl that works here? Her father told me she was working in this prison! I have awful timing. I wanted to see her again but not so soon! Now she's going to see me dirty and hungry. And I thought it wasn't possible to make a fool of myself so often!

I turn to Crooks, finally voicing my question.

"That girl wouldn't happen to be the daughter of the -

"BLUMENTHALS!" we both say at the same time.

"You already know her?" he asks, surprised. "Lucky you."

"Yes, I do," I reply. "For the better or worse."

Just the thought of Snowphia's blue eyes is enough to ease my pain. My heart starts beating fast when I think of how different everything would be if we'd met under different circumstances. Better circumstances. It hadn't even occurred to me that being locked up in this wretched place would give me the chance to see her again. Thanks to Charlie the Nutter, I had a feeling I'd spend a lot more time seeing her. There is always a silver lining to every situation.

"I got an initiation just like yours some weeks ago. But they can't get to me - you know why?"

I shake my head and cringe at the damage Charlie's gigantic foot had done to it.

"Because I am not afraid of pain or death," Crooks continues. "I'm afraid to die alone."

Being in prison makes you vulnerable. It seems to be one huge hate letter society has written to an unfortunate few, saying that prisoners are not loved, nor do they deserve to be. I've always assumed that if you are in a place like this, it means you have to act and look tough. But here is a man I've never met in my life and already, I know his deepest fear. Perhaps he knows that unless you are his friend, you can never hurt him.

"Time can heal pain and death - but it cannot heal loneliness. If you are alone today or in many years' time, the feeling is the same - you are all alone."

I nod at his statement. Boy, do I know a thing or two about loneliness. One of the many benefits of being in jail is that you have the chance to reflect on living alone. I mean, truly alone. Not in the company of ravens, deer, monkeys, and other loyal pets to comfort and converse with me. Crooks, if that is his real name, has clearly had his fair share of brutal loneliness. I consider telling him the real reason I've come back to Hamelin, but that isn't something I am going to say out loud with Charlie right next to me, tugging on his chains like a caged beast on the verge of breaking free.

"Well, there is a place where you can be happy alone," I say, not even able to turn my sore neck towards Crooks as I speak.

"And where is that?"

"Guernsey!"

"I have never heard of that place."

"And you never will. It's not on the map. It's a magical island. I spend my time there amid gardens full of every flower you can imagine, trees as tall as the mountains, and a sea so blue, you can see your own reflection. And I have a variety of pets, all who actually understand and help me. You'd think it was paradise."

"Oh yeah? Tell me more."

I'm surprised that he believes me. I know Crooks will be the first human friend I've had in a long time. After listening for a while (surprisingly, he's very sympathetic, for a man that has been treated so poorly) he starts telling me all about the prison (some men are bad, others don't want to be annoyed but won't kill you and Charlie is just another victim).

Most of those things can be easily gathered by looking around us with a critic eye and noticing the sheer lack of violent fights except when provoked by the most violent criminals. But most people are here for petty crimes, such as Crooks is.

"I was a regular man living my life and then the kids went missing and the animals happened and I found myself feeling hungry all the time and, without any money to buy food or anything to plant, I had no option but to steal. Mind you, I've never indulged in petty theft, I'm a simple fellow with a taste for cheap fruit and fish and I couldn't even afford the simplest food. It was a mess, it's still a mess. I've heard so much about you, but frankly, I wasn't expecting someone that looks so distinguished to be a criminal. You have well manners, and I'm sure you're very kind and even smell good when you're not in a hole like this," he says rather thoughtfully.

I can't help but feel my heart warming to the man and at the same time, I wonder if I truly reek. Now Snowphia is going to see me as liar, a killer and a man whose stench is even noticed by fellow prisoners.

He looks at me and gives me a small smile.

"The food here is terrible, sir. I think if you have magic you should do something about this situation. But I think, deep-down, you're a better man than our friends here," he says drawling the word 'friends' as if he wanted to say something else.

I sigh and look at my hands. If I could do something with them or my voice alone, that would be enough to break me out of here, but what happens if I also set free everyone here? It's a risky operation.

If only it was that easy!

From across the room, another prisoner starts to speak. In the darkness, I can't make out anything else except for his two eyes and the rusty shackles around his wrists.

"Everyone in here is a better man than the stupid Pied Piper, and you know why?"

Right, we've been speaking too loudly. The rest of the prisoners look at him with empty expressions, probably more interested in their own survival than the man's petty verbal aggression.

"These men have killed many of their fellow men, but they have never killed a woman or child. They are not cowards like the Pied Piper here - they do not attack people who are innocent or cannot defend themselves."

"A crime is a crime," Charlie hisses back. His breath reeks and I turn away as he speaks.

"So, are you saying I am a coward for beating up every man weaker than myself?"

"Oh, you are the exception."

"Shut up! He is the exception! You have just called Charlie a coward," Crooks reproaches.

"Oh no," cries the man, as he slumps back in the corner.

As the conversation proceeds, Charlie confesses that he was a cannibal. He'd gone to the tavern one day and gotten so drunk that he provoked a fight with a man. The result: Charlie ended up butchering him. When he discarded the body, he decided to take a chunk of flesh from the thigh, cook it over an open fire, and taste it. Mind you, Charlie hadn't eaten well in months. In morbid detail, he describes to us how boiled human flesh is flavourless to the palate, but roasting it gives it just the right juiciness. Worse over, he even fed some of the human meat to his neighbour and their family!

Bile rises in my throat while I struggle to maintain a straight face. I wonder how much of his story is true, and how much of it is just to instil fear in me. His vacant expression and sinister smile as he tells us what he did is enough to produce me -and anyone sensitive- nightmares for a lifetime, and he seems to be eager to give us more details about his kills.

I'm no amateur when it comes to yarns, myself. It is only when I hear such confessions that I am convinced I do not belong here. I'm chained next to a monster devoid of love. I still have love inside of me. That alone makes me innocent.

"D-do you enjoy the initiation process?" I hesitantly ask. I suppose I'm only trying to further prove my point.

"It's a release for me. All the anger inside of me comes out - I find it very spiritual."

Now that's not something I ever thought I'd hear. It's evil, I want to say how evil it is and how twisted and repulsive I find it and make him snap out of the weird trance he seems to be in, but here I am. Quiet and thinking of a way out of this aberrant place.

He laughs, small and eerie, almost like a child smile, but far more sinister- and he talks to me. A few more initiations, and Charlie would be Charlie the Monk! I guess in an odd way, Captain Hook figures he's providing him a twisted type of therapy.

"Oh, but you're a little Prince. You are surely disgusted at my antics and wish you didn't have to hear anything about me eating flesh. I bet you hate the prison food too." He comes near me and looks directly into my eyes.

"But I don't think you're a true Prince, a Prince wouldn't take children. I can't imagine you taking away any children if you're so nice and charming. No, I don't think that's the proper behaviour for a little Prince. You are an imposter, sir. A liar, and a killer, and its time you stop pretending otherwise," he said looking at me angrily. "Why don't you set us free then? Huh? You should be able to do so, what with your fancy flute and your wicked magic, but here you are, sitting and lamenting."

He slams the cell door as Captain Hook comes to collect him for the regular round of tortures and intimidation techniques. I turn to Crooks and he gives me a look of pity.

"I don't think he knows why you're here. He's a puppet. A dark, twisted and insanely strong puppet. Don't let it get to you."

His eyes are glinting and warm. He says I'm not to blame but I don't think he means it completely. After all, I have changed his life.

"I do wonder why you haven't broken us out yet," he says conversationally.

"I don't like the idea of setting him and other criminals free. What if we escape and he escapes too? He'll be eating innocent people! It doesn't matter if I escape and attempt to set anything right. We'll all be better off dead than having Charlie outside, free to torment anyone."

With that, he regards me briefly and I look at him calmly.

"I wouldn't think of it that way. You shouldn't ever abandon hope," says Crooks and pats me in the arm. A man I don't know is showing more kindness than my people ever did...

I wonder if I'll ever be able to repay his kindness. I certainly wish I could go back to the way everything was. Am I destined to be uprooted from my people? I wish doing things my way didn't result in so much heartbreak. If being who I am is a source of trouble for everyone, then I don't want to be true to myself.

Oh, how I miss my home and the extremely well-kept hallways of school. I miss them more than the castle.

*

"Tomorrow, there's a prison visit. You'll spend time with Snowphia who will nurse your wounds," Hook informs me before resting his head against the cold wall to go to sleep.

Just the thought lifted my spirits. A shining light, in a very dark place.

I drift into a comforting slumber.

"Wake up!" someone whispers.

I pull open my eyelids and blink a few times. "Wake up!"

Who is talking to me? Charlie is snoring to my left, and Crooks is snoring even louder to my right. The man across from me is completely motionless, fast asleep.

"Its Sherbert! Up here!"

"And Pepe, don't forget about me!" chirps Pepe happily.

I look above me and realize he must be at the window ledge.

"Hey, you!" I whisper back. What a pleasant surprise.

"How did you get yourself holed up in here?"

"It's long story." I try to keep as quiet as possible, so the cannibal next to me doesn't wake up. "Can you get me out of here?"

"How?"

"There's a forest I was taken to by a mysterious man - you can perhaps go there and ask him to help me. He seemed to know a lot about who I am."

Yes, he did know a lot. Because of what they told them. I want to point out the fact that I feel like they are behind some of this chaos. However, I don't have the heart to fight with them. They came here after all. And I'm still an animal lover and they're my beloved friends.

"If there is anyone who knows their way around the world, then it is us - I can assure you there is no forest within this region!"

My heart sinks.

Am I imagining all this?

"Come back tomorrow. I will think of something."

And tomorrow, I will figure out whether Sherbert was really here or if it was just a dream. What's actually important is that talking to Sherbert and Pepe has made me realize I still have the will to plan a way out of this place. I will escape without harming anyone and maybe my heroic act will be able to wash off some of my sins. If I free Crooks, he will be given the justice he can't achieve on his own. But how? Without my magic, I'll have to be clever.

CHAPTER 10

THE MUSIC MAGICIAN

"Rise and shine, darling!" someone shouts in my direction. Considering I have Charlie the Nutter sleeping to my left and Crooks sleeping to my right, the only person the voice is possibly addressing is me. Seconds later, I'm drenched in cold ice water.

Oh, if he knew how much I hate that.

But then again, I think if he truly knew how much it bothers me to be surrounded by brutes and having to hear his lovely voice every morning, he'd start enjoying himself.

"Someone wants to see you right now," he continues. What are the chances I refuse and go back to sleep, now that I'm wet, cold, and angry?

"Hurry up," the impatient voice prompts.

It's so dark that I still can't see where the voice is coming from. I'm sure it's one of the Gustavos, considering he has the nerve to throw cold water on me.

But whoever it is appears to be afraid of waking Charlie. The nutter is still snoring in a deep sleep, drool dripping from his open mouth as his head rests on his shackled arm. Sometimes I wish I were as intimidating as him, so the prisoners and guards would just leave me alone.

The abrupt wake up still catches me off guard, and a million thoughts swim through my head. I follow the source of the voice out of the dungeon, my soaked long black hair leaving a trail of water on the stone floor.

Just when I think they'll give me a robe; they hand me the stupid blindfold again. I cross my arms, shivering miserably in the cold morning air. Worse over, it's windy, and the sting of the cold is even more painful than the wounds from the previous day. I begin to wonder if I'll catch influenza before I even reach the Diele.

"I will be quick," says a voice that sounds familiar, gasping for air as if he's just sprinted across the city. It's the Mayor. It amazes me that in a small town that is supposedly starving, the Mayor is somehow getting fatter and fatter by the day. I'm surprised he's managed to drag his plump self out of bed this early. I know it must be important.

"Listen and listen very carefully, I am giving you ONE last chance to redeem yourself - you HEAR?" He warns me, snorting as he inhales a few times to catch his breath.

"Everyone thinks you killed the children, but is there any chance that they are miraculously still alive and you can bring them back?"

I am gobsmacked. Here he is again, trying to cheat me for the second time.

"It should be you in these chains and not me!" I snap indignantly, pointing a finger at him. "I am the one who saved the town, you are the one who lied! How about we start from there?"

The Mayor whacks me across the head with all his might. His weak fist feels like no more than a pebble hitting my temple, but it's enough to make my tired legs slip to the ground. I feel him bend down and press his dry lips to the edges of my ear. At least they were warm.

"Do you want to know what I want?" he spits. I can feel the warm saliva slowly worming its way to my eardrum. I shudder a bit.

"I will have your head on a stake and your body will light up our bonfire."

He pushes me to the ground, and I hear him scurry away from me.

"Take him back inside!" he shouts from a distance.

***

It's a few hours before all the prisoners will be woken up. I'm still fuming at the Mayor's sheer audacity to ask for the children back, so I find myself unable to fall back asleep.

I stare into the darkness, hoping the boredom will lull me to sleep. There are no stars to count, so I decide to try reminiscing about my life back in Guernsey. I wonder how little Boris is doing, hoping he hasn't gotten too lonely. My thoughts turn to Hemlock Fair Nostrils and Chuka. They're in good hands with Snowphia, so I'm confident they'll okay. But Fatso is another story – I'm worried about how he's faring out there all by himself.

"Rise and shine, darling." At first, I'm convinced it's déjà vu.

Today is just not my day. I wearily pull myself up and blink a few times to adjust my eyes to the light streaming in through the window above.

"Good boy - you learn quickly, don't you?" teases the voice.

As the sun starts to rise, I can see the Gustavo who's speaking to me. He's a short man with a thick moustache planted across his face and a grin that shows he's enjoying himself far more than any of us. I glance down at him, as he's nearly half my size, but he gives my wrists a violent tug to reinforce who's boss.

"Sister Leola Agnes Ploughbag from the St. Nicholai Church is here to see you. Be on your best behaviour."

I nod as if I care. I'm more interested in knowing why a nun is visiting me than anything else.

"Guten tag," she greets in a soft voice.

I keep quiet. It's too early to go through all the niceties.

"Will you join me in prayer before we talk?" she asks me. It must be a rhetorical question. I'm tired, broken, and in chains, so I'll have to go along with anything she asks me to do.

"Sie," I reply as I bow my head and close my eyes. I brace myself.

"Dear Lord, I bring this sinful child of yours before you this morning," she begins. I glance over at her with one eye open, in disbelief at her speech.

"Before he dies, open his heart, imprison his pride, and release the shackles from his humility so that he may confess his sins and avoid the eternal scourge of Satan's fork!"

I'm flabbergasted. Not only am I to suffer while in prison, but another never-ending punishment awaits me in hell.

"Amen," she closes the prayer.

"Danke," I say in a low voice, not wanting to not show gratitude.

She proceeds to sit down on the nearby bench and places a large metal cross on the table.

"Will you be confessing your sins, my son?" she asks softly.

"What sins?" I retort.

"Confess your sins," she demands.

"What sins?"

"Confess your SINS," she demands again, this time louder than before.

"Tell me what sins and I will confess them."

"Confess your SINS," she shouts at me as she bangs the cross on the table.

"Before I confess any sins, may I know why the church has not taken down my picture on the stained glass?"

"That is none of your business. Those are church matters," she snaps.

"Don't take your churches being full as a sign that people love you - they are just running away from their sufferings."

"I haven't the slightest idea what you're talking about," she grumbles, probably not having listened to a word I've said. "CONFESS YOUR SINS!"

"If I confess my sins, what happens then?"

"Your sins will be forgiven, but considering the depth of your sins, you'll have to pay an indulgence towards the church," she says with a straight face.

"A what?" I ask, amazed.

"Some sins cannot be wiped away just by a mere confession. You will have to pay based on the kind of sin, or someone else pays it for you." It's as if God will use the money to renovate heaven and hell!

"Can I nominate the Mayor to pay the thousand gold coins he owes me as my indulgence?" I try hard not to laugh.

She pauses as if taking seriously what I've said. "May your soul burn a thousand times in hell and may Satan's fork pluck out that heart of stone you have inside," she shouts as she pokes my chest with her sharp, thin fingers.

The nun gets up and leaves, just like that. She stops to speak to one of the Gustavo lingering outsides of the church, apparently waiting for me. I can just about hear their discussion.

"There is no hope even in hell for this arrogant fool."

"Sorry, ma'am - the Pied Piper is a lost cause. He is a troubled man."

"SISTER, before you leave!" I exclaim. She only stops in her tracks because I imagine she thinks I'm about to offer her the gift of my confession.

"When children die, where do they go?" I ask her.

"To heaven of course," she snarls.

"If I have sent them to a better place like heaven – shouldn't you and the parents be thanking me instead?"

Her eyes become blood red.

She whacks my face with the cross.

I ache badly. Who could imagine a nun to be so strong? She had more force in her blow than even the Mayor! I sit on the floor and patiently wait for Snowphia to come in and dress my wounds.

"Rise and shine," the short man shouts again. I'm boiling with anger at the sight of him. Bring in Snowphia already!

"What now?" I grumble. I'm half expecting a beating of some sort. It's been that kind of morning that all the worst possible scenarios collide in a period of hours. Even nuns have had a go at me.

Maybe I'm just not a morning person. He pokes at my wounds with his truncheon. It hurts more than the beatings. I wince in pain.

"Ok!" I choke out. "I'm sorry." I get up and trail behind him.

"You will be having a meeting with Lez," he says, stopping by a door to let me in.

"What a pleasure to finally meet you, Mr. Piper," Lez greets me, taking out a few sheets of notes and a feathered quill. He pushes his glasses up the bridge of his nose, maintaining a grave expression that brings me nothing but unease.

"Do you want a confession out of me?" I ask him.

"You read my mind like a fortune teller, sir," he replies with a nervous smile, perhaps half-suspecting I'm a serial killer.

"Ever since I've heard about the story of the missing children, I've taken on the burden of trying to help the parents find out what happened to them. They need closure and it's my responsibility to give them that."

He pulls out a stack of newspapers from his leather pouch and drops them on the table with a thud.

"As you can see here, I have been investigating and writing stories about what could have happened to the children, but none of the theories have helped with closure. After all, they want to know what happened, not just what could have happened. And since the very child thief is here in the flesh, perhaps a confession of what happened to the missing children could redeem you and help the families."

He dips his quill in the inkwell.

"I am going to read some of my possible theories - if I strike the right chord, let me know."

I'm convinced he's more interested in showing off his own cleverness than actually facilitating my testimony. Is this a multiple-choice exam or something?

"Theory number one - this one seems probable. You led the children on some sort of crusade?"

"Nope," I say.

He scrapes a check next to the "#1" on his parchment.

"Ok, theory number two is that you killed them all." He looks up at me and pushes up his circle glasses again, his face tense. Yes, he apparently must think I'm a serial killer. Did he really expect me to agree with him?

"Nope."

Lez breathes a sigh of relief.

"Are you absolutely sure you did not kill those innocent children?"

"Whether I did or not, there is no witness, so my answer means nothing," I reason.

"You're right, but now that you're in prison, you have nothing to lose in telling the truth."

I begin to wonder if he's even a journalist at all. It seems that all morning, I've been forced to cough up false confessions.

"Theory number three -," Lez clears his throat. "You played your flute for some long hours consecutively, possibly for three days, and the children, hypnotized by the sounds, fell to the ground, tired from the dancing mania. Consequently, you disposed of the bodies in some hidden place."

I raise my eyebrow. Is he serious? His theories are getting even more outlandish, and I start to wonder if he's the madman in this room!

"No, again?" he confirms, seemingly already losing faith in his theories.

"I would drop dead myself if I played my flute for three days straight."

He nods and puts a check next to it on his parchment to rule it out.

"Alright," Lez sighs. "Theory number four - you led them to the bridge above the river, which collapsed, resulting in their drowning. Induced or not induced by dancing mania."

"Nope," I click. I don't even bother expressing my surprise this time.

He checks it off the bottom of his list and turns to the next sheet of notes. Is he kidding? The theories go on for more than one page?

"Theory number five -."

"Just stop with all these theories." I shake my head in ridicule. "The children are not dead, but I cannot bring them back, wherever they are." My tone is resolute. I no longer want to continue the conversation. I'm exhausted, cold, and in pain from the early morning rendezvous, and quite honestly would rather curl up and go back to sleep than be put through any more interrogations.

"If they are not dead, then, where are they?" he asks. He pulls out my flute from his pouch and sets it on the table. "Perhaps you can lure them back with this?"

"It doesn't work like that - they have to be able to HEAR ME to follow me," I say with an eye roll. I'm shocked how little Earthlings know about music magicians!

"Have you ever heard about music magicians?" I ask him, knowing full well he will assume we are some weird wizards that use music to cast spells.

"You mean you are a wizard but plays music instead," Lez replies, walking right into it like a typical Earthling!

My eyes almost rolled out the back of my head. This is probably how Captain Hook lost his eye!

"You were saying?" I urge him to continue. There is no point explaining to him the wonderful world of a music magician.

"So, why come back to Hamelin?" He leans in towards me, pointing the feather of his quill at my nose in accusation. "Why come back disguised as a Prince? Unless you are one sick evil bastard that came back to steal more children?"

He stares into my eyes from behind his glossy lenses, as if trying to threaten me.

"Is it money that you want from us? Are you still trying to make us pay for how we wronged you earlier?"

"Huh?"

"Answer me, greedy money grabber!" he raises his voice.

Lez gets up and starts pouring coins onto the floor.

"Is this what you want - is this what it takes to have our children back and rid of you forever?" he exclaims.

I sit there in silence. What am I supposed to say?

"Excuse me, sir," a sweet voice interrupts, "could I attend to Mr. Piper's wounds?"

I twist around and look behind me. It's Snowphia, standing by the doorway with a cloth in one hand and a dish of warm water in the other.

***

"I'm not sure why you bother to nurse this vile man back to health," Lez grumbles as he packs his wares to leave.

"Charlie!" Captain Hook shouts while walking down the hallway. "You're no longer the most popular with the young ladies of Hamelin!" He chuckles maliciously. "The new Mr. Hamelin is the infamous Pied Piper!"

I hear my name and look up. Captain Hook is pacing about as he proceeds to slander me.

"It seems that news of your incarceration has reached all four corners of Hamelin rather quickly and is bedazzling the young women! Who knew that evil could be attractive?"

"Those stupid whores!" Charlie affirms, his voice echoing down the hallway.

Upon hearing this, Snowphia seems to slow her pace as she approaches. She examines the wounds on my face and dips the cloth in the water.

"This may sting a bit," she warns me.

The saltwater is pleasantly warm, but I cringe at the way it burns.

"Everyone here hates me," I mutter, trying to attract at least a hint of her empathy.

"Prisoners are good at hating one another," she replies.

"The whole town hates me, I should correct."

She's silent. I guess it means I'm right. My heart can't sink any lower. I have no doubt that she'll never love a man like me.

Though, I can try anyway.

"What the Captain's shouting isn't true," I blurt out. "I don't even know any of the young women of Hamelin. Except for you."

"For the better," she replies.

I can't help but pull a proud smirk at the remark.

"I – I mean, the kinds of women here who fall for prisoners are damaged goods," she explains. "They are not the people you'd want to interact with."

"Are you saying I don't belong here?"

She looks at me but offers no reply.

"Hold out your arm," she finally instructs.

I shiver as she pulls up my sleeve to examine the wounds. I'm not sure if it's the cold, or the gentle tickle of her fingertips.

"Or you're just saying you'd never fall for a prisoner," I correct.

This time Snowphia doesn't even look at me. She proceeds to dab the wounds with the wet cloth. Somehow the stinging of the saltwater doesn't affect me anymore. I'm not sure if it's because of the comfort of her touch, or that her seemingly silent affirmation stings more.

Snowphia takes a deep breath, gesturing for me to hold out my other arm.

"I've come across many personalities in my time here," she begins. "I have heard many twisted confessions. I've even feared for my life. And never would my family allow a single one of these madmen to cross the threshold of our doorstep. My father is no fool. He saw something special in you. It was the way you walked in here with your magical pets and a sack of toys. It was something in your soul. You're unique, different, if I might add, sir, but not evil or corrupted in any way. My father didn't sense that on you, and I've been trying to find something wrong with you, but I can't," she says, blushing slightly.

I can hardly believe my ears.

"I don't know what has happened to Maddie. I don't know where she is, or if she will come back. But I also do not believe the lies this town invents. And I'm not sure I believe a word of what they are saying about you."

My mouth falls open. She is the only person in this town that even hints at my goodness.

"Mr. Piper – why not seek redemption?"

"Redemption?" I repeat, not quite understanding.

"You came back here. Why not bring the children with you? Why not bring Maddie back to us?"

I bow my head solemnly, sadness washing over me. I regret that I don't have an answer for her, or simply am bereft of the courage to muster the words to explain.

"I don't know where you come from," she continues. "Or how the mysterious power of your music works. But surely you knew this town wouldn't welcome you with open arms. So, I have to ask, Mr. Piper, one question that has haunted me since they told me you were here, in this prison – Hamelin's prison. Why did you come back, if not for redemption?"

I part my lips to speak, but not a sound comes out.

"Do you want the honest answer? Or a safe lie?" I finally ask.

"We have enough lies here in Hamelin."

"Fair enough. I – I," I stutter. "Let me start from the beginning. Day in and day out, my pets listened to me speak of my loneliness. So, my ravens set out to find me a companion."

"Your pets understand you?" she laughs. "And you have ravens?"

"Effectively – yes."

She giggles like a little girl at my seeming tall tale. It warms my heart to see her smile.

"They returned to me after a fortnight and said they had found the perfect woman. Generous, kind, humble – beautiful. This woman fed them bread when they were starving. But the drawback – she lives in Hamelin."

Snowphia squints dubiously. "You're a storyteller alright, Mr. Piper."

Suddenly, she stops her motions, letting the cloth fall into the water, floating. Something is on her mind.

"The ravens," she mutters to herself. Agape, she looks up at me, finally having connected the dots.

"Snowphia," I plead. "I came back here for you."

Snowphia gives me one last look with her large, striking eyes, and stands up with the bowl of water in her hands.

"Please excuse me," she gasps, before darting out of the room.

Well. That didn't go as planned. But it also went better than it could have, considering the circumstances.

"Beware!" I hear from outside the room. It's Lez's voice, who apparently is still lingering in the hallway. The castle walls seem to amplify everything – there are no secrets here!

"He is like a snake that will beguile you," Lez warns her. "Before you know it, you'll have been bitten and poisoned by his charms. Those children were not forced to come with him – they followed him. And he will do the same to you."

***

After all the humiliations I have endured and Snowphia's rejection, I find myself seeking Crook's company, he's my only friend here and I like the idea of talking to him since he's a good listener.

Maybe its best I try telling him about music magicians. He has an inquisitive mind; he makes the perfect audience.

I start of by telling him about the beautiful, hidden castle with the mysterious doors and rooms. How I almost fell down a window trying to reach for a raven that had a broken wing. How, other Pied Pipers just like me, were likely to get into trouble and give until people abused their tendency to want to help.

I tell him about Lucifarians, Jacksons, Pied Pipers, and Davidians, Azwan's four famous music tribes. He instantly picks up on the first ones being almost always evil and I nod along. They got their name from Lucifer, who, most believe, oversaw all the music in heaven. Then, I explain that Jacksons and Davidians use music to provide entertainment and healing, respectively.

"I was almost a Davidian myself. They're skilled at taking care of others and I've always been bad at putting myself first. With me, it seems I'm always the last choice and the first to be hurt."

"You ought to learn better then, Your Highness," he utters mockingly but without any poison on his voice.

I let out a dry laugh and continue with my tale.

"The Pied Pipers are the good music magicians. To be one you must have a good heart."

"That's good, there's no risk our friend Hook will secretly be a Piper," he says grimacing.

I laugh higher this time.

"You're going to get us into trouble," I say quietly, composing myself.

"We –Pied Pipers- make sure people are helped, but unlike Davidians, we use magic to help out those in trouble. Where a Davidian would heal, we just help out, in whatever way we can."

"And that's it?" he asks. "And this means you're also something else. Your name can hardly be Pied Piper if there's a bunch of us around anyway. And what's an Earthling?"

"Lucifarians are worshipers of gods which act power-hungry at their worst and almighty at their worst. One of them had my nose broken when I had the bravery to tell him off for attacking a female Earthling that couldn't defend herself under the sheer power of his magic. My nose hasn't been the same since then," I say grimacing, ignoring his question about Earthlings.

He looks at me bewildered.

"And what about the term Earthling? What is that about?" he insists.

I sigh.

"Do not take this the wrong way, an Earthling is simply a person without musical talent. They can't cast any magic using music. You'd be called an Earthling back home if they ever got to know you."

There is an implicit question hanging between. He doesn't know who 'them' are. But I'm not about to tell him explicitly. It is for his own good.

He voices them very quickly.

"I don't think you want to speak about it, but I'm guessing you're, in fact, not telling me the whole story. You claim that you're a Prince, but you're here, alone, and no one has come to your aid. Did you do something bad at home? Something that made you run away and land here?" I can't believe how sharp he is. Maybe he has the solution to escaping this damned place!

"Alright, since it's evident that it's going to be you and me only for the longest time, I'm going to tell you the story of the worst thing I've ever done."

His eyes are wide open as he looks at me, but he manages to regain composure as I continue my tale.

"Not so long ago, a Pied Piper named Kissenga, Prince of Azwan was faced with the decision of making his friends slaves to his people. He didn't want that to happen, so he decided to escape as far away as his magical flute and his sharp abilities would allow. His motivations weren't as strong before, but once he faced ridicule from the whole court, including those he cared the most about, he decided that there wasn't a place for him there anymore. Nor for his companions. He did all sort of spells. Magic is the transfixing and re-shaping of matter, essentially, so he took a disguise, changed his outfit slightly and took his magical instruments –and his friends- and that was all the company he needed. But then, he heard a nation's call, he felt empathy for those that were suffering under what they perceived as a plague and the horrors the small, innocent 'pests' suffered, and he took pity on them. I took them under my wing by playing the Pipe; the children weren't part of the plan!"

I sag slowly and throw myself against the wall almost violently. A bitter sob escapes my throat, but he doesn't complain. Prison changes the smallest things for people. Besides, he must have witnessed quite a few people breaking like this. I start complaining about the unfortunate course of my even more unfortunate run in with the nun and before I can stop myself, I'm telling him the truth. That I am the Prince of Azwan, that I live with my animal companions and that I couldn't ever hurt an animal or any sentient being.

He looks at me and –sighing- he speaks.

"Why are you so worried about this then? I'm sure you'll be able to break free of here. At least you have a better outlook than the rest of us."

"Yes, but you know it isn't quite so easy for me. I have tried time and time again for things to be better and now, I'm here suffering. I wish people wouldn't seek to destroy me in every step of the road."

He looks at me and nods.

"It's true. Although, you don't strike me as someone that has suffered hunger or poverty, I can tell that you've lived a difficult life. But you can't let this get the better of you. You must escape this place and bring justice to our land! Make everything that's happening a bad, bitter memory, and win over that woman you've been yearning to have and cherish her every day, for the rest of your life."

"We're all going to die!" says Crooks. "What matters is how we want to be remembered when we are gone. Unfortunately, it seems we're bound to be remembered as a thief and a child thief!"

"I don't think that's quite as simple. I wish it was as simple as that. I'm punished for not doing things the way my father wanted me to. I'm being punished unfairly for not letting my people enslave who they want. And you want to know something else? I'm also guilty of the children's disappearance. I'm sure they took the children away from their parents as a punishment. Now I can see things the way they are."

"I'm sure my destiny is to die here in Hamelin under the guillotine, that's the prize for thinking of others before me and for not thinking enough how things would turn out after using my flute. How I would do to understand how everything would turn out before it is happening, I don't know, but it's a fact: I've made the worst mistake of my life."

He gives me a wide-eyed look and I lower my gaze. What he doesn't know is that I'm already thinking of what I'm going to do about this. And it isn't going to be easy, but I'll manage to achieve what I want, even if it's the last thing I do.

CHAPTER 11

A SECRET LOVE

"My darling daughter, you must be unwell - do you know what time it is?" Mr. Blumenthal remarked as he opened the curtains in Snowphia's room.

"I have a fever, Papa, and I do not think I can go to the prison today."

"I would love to believe you, my dear, but you know your mother," he warned her. Ever since losing Maddie, Mrs. Blumenthal had become an obsessive worrier. A little cough here and there, and she became convinced it was a knock at death's door.

"Please don't tell her I am unwell."

"I won't have to - you will have to explain it yourself."

"My dear daughter, how bad is it?" the feeble Mrs. Blumenthal asked, shuffling into the room, and sitting at Snowphia's bedside. She had been eavesdropping on their conversation.

"Oh Mama, I thought I was unwell, but just seeing your face makes me feel better," Snowphia fibbed to ease her mother's concern.

"Oh!"

"Well, I better get to work," Mr. Blumenthal excused himself, slipping on his wool cloak. "The Mayor is determined to make an example of the Pied Piper and it is taking more planning than I had anticipated."

"Did you say the Pied Piper?" Mrs. Blumenthal asked in shock.

Mr. Blumenthal paused, realizing he had let slip something that would cause trouble in the household for the next few days. He hung his cloak back up, took a deep breath, and returned to Snowphia's room.

"My darling wife. I wanted you to know this nearer to Christmas." He placed a comforting hand on her shoulder. "We finally caught the Pied Piper and right now, he is in prison waiting for his execution. Finally, he'll pay for what he did to us all."

"My good Lord - so is Maddie back? Where is she?" Mrs. Blumenthal jumped up in a panic. "Where is she? Take me to her!"

Mr. Blumenthal just shook his head.

"The children are no more," he said.

"How do you know this? Has the Pied Piper confessed to killing them?" she panted.

"No, he has not."

"THEN, WHY KILL THE MAN?" Mrs. Blumenthal screamed at the top of her lungs.

Snowphia quietly slipped out of her bed, threw on her walking dress and went into the snowy town to retrieve Nurse Alice.

Nurse Alice arrived at once, firmly committed to her job that she was convinced only she, of all medical professionals in Hamelin, could do properly. She doused a white cloth with liquid from the Flask of Madness, and from behind, placed the cloth across Mrs. Blumenthal's face.

"Take me to the -" Mrs. Blumenthal slumped onto the floor.

"Oh, dear God, thank you!" Mr. Blumenthal said.

"She always looks beautiful when calm and asleep," remarked Snowphia as she helped Nurse Alice to drag Mrs. Blumenthal onto the bed.

"Papa, what if Mama is right? What if Maddie and the other children aren't dead? Why kill the Pied Piper?"

"Snowphia, your mom is unwell. She'll go even more mad if she's convinced that Maddie is alive."

"But what if she is alive? Yesterday a man came to question Mr. Piper and he denied killing them."

"Are you sure?"

"Yes!" she reaffirmed.

"So, why did the Pied Piper come back? And to think, I housed this vile man in my -"

"He's not vile!" Snowphia exclaimed.

"And now, he seems to have beguiled you too," said Mr. Blumenthal, as he got ready to put his cloak back on.

"Well, if you should know, I asked him why then he came back, and he told me it was for love."

"Love?"

"He came back for me!"

"WHAT?" Mr. Blumenthal ripped open the door. "I am going to go to that prison this very moment and I am going to damn well kill him myself."

"Papa, now you're the madman! Just think about it. He came and stayed with us. He ate with us and kept apologising when you told him about Mama. Why else would a man of such infamy come back here?"

Snowphia sighed, convinced her father's prejudice would never subside.

"He was sincere when he told me about it. I just didn't know what to say to him today. That's why I feigned illness this morning."

Mr. Blumenthal took a seat, trying to collect his wits so he could talk his daughter into being more sensible. "Part of me wants to believe that our dear Maddie is still alive, but having lived with your mother all these years, perhaps her folly has found its way unto us all and now we find ourselves sympathising with the man who took her away?"

"Papa, let me go back to the prison and hear him out." Snowphia implored. "Besides, why would he lie when he is about to die?"

***

"I thought you would never come back," I murmur, looking up from the rotting, wooden table in the visitor's room. It's amazing that medical treatment is given in this chamber, considering it's just as cold, musty, and dark as the dungeon.

"Why would you think that?" Snowphia replies prosaically, sitting down with her bowl of warm saltwater.

"Because of the way you abruptly left the last time -"

"I was unwell this morning," she cuts me off defensively.

"And do you feel better now that you have seen me?" I say with a cheeky smile.

She takes my arm, pushes up the sleeve, and presses the cloth to the bloody bruise. I cringe at the sudden sting. Am I being punished for having a sense of humour?

"Not only are you a skilled nurse, but playful too."

"Or I can just leave." She looks me in the eye, pursing her lips in frustration.

"Why are you being short with me today?"

I'm afraid she's convinced I'm the awful man the town is accusing me of being. Of all people, I don't want her to believe that. Deep down inside, I feel vulnerable. How many long, lonely days have I spent ruminating on my remorse for what I've done? Is that not enough? When all along, I know I've saved the town from a demise they couldn't even fathom?

"Look, its miserable within these four walls," I explain. "All day, my nostrils are filled with the foul air. I must sleep next to two snoring buffoons all evening. And I am still hurting from the beatings - you are the only good thing that happens to me."

"I'm glad to know I am an object that satisfies," she drones. "There I was, thinking I was useless."

What was wrong with her today? How could telling her I've come to this wretched Hamelin just for her make her so bitter towards me?

Then again, I haven't brushed my teeth in days, nor have they allowed me to bathe or shave, so that could be part of it. And there is also the possibility that she is feeling pushed by my attitude. I just can't help but feel drawn to her. Not only is she beautiful on the outside, the very depths of her soul call to mine. I feel it like a pull. It's greater than the pull magic can make on its casters. It's far harder to refrain myself from feeling close to her and interested in getting closer and closer until we're inexorably joined.

"I mean it. You're the only one who understands me, who I can actually converse with like a human being. It's a blessing to be with you, trust me. I've never felt something like this before. I've always felt so utterly alone, and now, I have you. I don't mean it as you being my property. When I say I have you, what I mean is that we have each other. Until you'll have me, I'll be here for you. Can't you see my intentions don't have malicious intent, Snowphia?"

Snowphia's lips tremble, as if she wants to smile but is unable. I feel a lump starting to form in my throat.

"If you should know why I am like this," she says dolefully, "it's because of Mama. For the first time in months, she relapsed the moment she heard you were back in town. If it weren't for Alice, she might have assaulted Papa again. She was convinced that you came back with Maddie."

"Oh," I nod, bowing my head in shame. "I'm sorry."

"Well, the damage is done now. I don't know how long she'll be like this. It could be months or even years before she starts to recover again."

Snowphia gently dabs the wounds on my face. I'm relieved to feel some level of tenderness from her despite how upset she is with me.

"I can help."

She doesn't even look at me. I'm sure it means she doesn't believe me.

"How can you do that?" Snowphia continues patting my face as if I were a sick, helpless infant. "You'll be gone sooner than we think," she says and then winces. "Forgive me, that was cold. What I meant is that your destiny is uncertain at best and cursed at worst…"

"I can marry you and your father can use the money to pay for your mother's care."

Snowphia retreats the cloth and submerges it in the water. I seem to have broken the spell.

"How dare you say such things when discussing a serious matter?" she retorts.

"Look, I am going to die anyway. Why let the money rot in the hills when I can actually help your mother?"

"Oh. So, money solves everything now?" Snowphia pushes herself up from the chair, preparing to leave me just like that, all over again. "If it weren't for your love of money, everything would still be fine."

"You really believe that?"

"YES! I don't care where you come from or why you came back, but money's not everything. Fine, let's say, God forbid, I marry you. We get the money. Nurse Alice will tend to Mama for maybe a few years. Will Mama ever forget about Maddie? Will she one day be a normal loving wife to Papa or a loving mother to me?"

"Listen to me very carefully - I know you're angry right now but what I did with those children saved this whole town - it saved your mother, your father and you."

It's unfortunate wording. I know it is, but since we're speaking so heatedly, I can't help but say whatever comes out of my mind first. Now she thinks I'm proud of killing, or making the children disappear.

"What do you mean? Are you so twisted in your mind that you believe kidnapping children for money somehow is a good thing for this town?"

Snowphia snatches the bowl and storms off towards the doorway. "Maybe what this town said about you was right after all. Not even death can make you see how much of a vile person you are."

My mouth drops open. I'm at a loss for words. Vile? Where is the serene, understanding Snowphia from yesterday?

"Call me what you like," I reply "Accuse me of all sorts. But hear me out."

I stand up, approaching her so she can witness the desperation in my eyes.

"My name isn't 'The Pied Piper'. That's a name that has to do with my magical abilities. My true name is Kissenga. I am not a simple Pied Piper. I come from a powerful family that rules the Nubian people in Azwan. Instead of fighting to consolidate my father's power, I chose to go on my own path. I spent my time in this kingdom, travelling around and helping cities in trouble. My father let me do this on one condition - that no one dishonours our family by letting others know my true name and heritage.

You see, the Mayor of Hamelin deceived me. When I left this town, if news of what the Mayor did to me had reached my father, the winged lions would have come to ravage Hamelin and everyone in it."

Snowphia stares at me wide-eyed, absorbing my words.

"I came back. And took the children instead and sold them to another powerful family who could protect them. I used the money to pay my father. When my family found out about what I had done - they banished me to Guernsey!"

"Azwan? I've never heard such a thing. Why should I believe you?"

I sigh, feeling defeated.

"Because even if you don't, it's still the truth."

"So, if you are from such a powerful family, then why are you still in prison waiting for your death?"

"I can summon the winged lions to come rescue me anytime - but they would destroy this place as well. No one in this kingdom can see them and live."

I reach my hand out and take hers. Her clammy, delicate fingers sink into my dirty palm. Miraculously, she doesn't pull away.

"I am enduring all this because of you," I continue. "I want you to come with me, so we can search for your sister and the rest of them too."

"But you've already sold them."

"I can get them back, even if it means risking a war between the families."

"And all for what - me, a mere peasant girl?"

"All for the kindest, fairest and most generous girl on this earth, peasant or not. Yes, all of your love and my redemption."

Only then do I notice she's wearing the pearl earrings I gifted her days before. It means something to me – the only value that materialism can serve.

"What has all this power and wealth got for me? I have spent many years in Guernsey with everything I could ever need. I have painted. Studied. Invented. I have discovered the world. But when I die - what good are all these accomplishments? What good is all my wealth? I would rather die having loved than never to have tasted what it is like to be in love."

Her hand falls from mine.

"But how can I love you? How can I love the very man who has destroyed my family? In that house, we are three desperately lonely people. Papa lost his wife that day. I lost both my parents. Papa doesn't even want to be loving towards me, fearing that I too will be taken away. And you expect me to love a prisoner facing a death sentence?"

"I am not asking you to love me today. I am asking you to let me plant the seeds of love in your heart. And I am asking you to give me a chance to water them and let your love for me grow inside of you. Could you grant that to me? Or will you leave, never to set eyes on me again?"

Snowphia shakes her head. "It's not like that _"

"I would conquer a thousand worlds for your love."

"I would rather you conquer your pride."

"Do you hate me? Like the rest of Hamelin? After all I have confessed to you?"

Snowphia pauses as if she's battling with what she feels and what she believes she should say. "I hate the fact that I do not hate you with the raging fire of a thousand suns."

"If you look into my eyes, you will see a thousand stories of my past, and of my heart that I cannot even begin to tell."

She gazes at me, tears gathering at the ducts of her blue eyes. Amidst them, I can read pity.

"I don't hate you," she murmurs again. A few tears drop from her eyes and stream down her cheek, and she wipes them away with the sleeve of her blouse. "That is why I ran away when you said you came to me."

"Come with me?"

Snowphia's head droops in contemplation. "I so badly want to believe you, Mr. Pip – um, Kissenga. I so badly want to believe all of this is true, that you are the saviour of Hamelin, not the enemy. I so badly want to believe that Maddie is safe, waiting for me to rescue her – waiting for us to bring her back. Bringing back the children would be the happiest day that Hamelin could ever experience."

I brush away a tear from her soft cheek with my weathered fingers. Then I hold out my upturned palm towards her, and she hesitantly rests her hand on it.

"But imagine me leaving with the infamous Pied Piper, what would it do to my Mama and Papa?"

"The plan is for your mother to never know until we return," I assure her. "Your father seems like a reasonable man and since he thinks I am going to die anyway; he will probably accept the marriage proposal. When we get out of this place, leave him a note that you have gone to look for Maddie."

"And you think it's that easy to have your daughter run off with the Pied Piper?"

"Look, my family by now probably knows of my fate. They are just awaiting my call for help or they will come at the last hour and rescue me anyway - but that would mean everyone including your father and mother will die too. I am asking you to come with me to save yourself, your mother, your father, and me!"

"What choice do I have?" she concedes.

"To stay and die together when the winged lions come for us, or to go and find your sister."

"Interesting proposition, Mr. Piper" Lez interrupts, slowly clapping as he invades the room.

"You really are a charmer. Even I would have let you run away with my daughter. Even with my wife. Only that I don't have a wife or daughter because I have dedicated my entire life to seeking justice for these heartbroken families. And here you are, charming your way into an innocent girl whose sister you so cruelly snatched away."

He clasps Snowphia's shoulders, seeing her off to the hallway. Her fingertips curl to keep hold of my hand before we're finally separated.

"Young woman, you are done here. Leave for the day."

Snowphia's scarf flutters through the air as she darts down the hallway and out of the prison.

I wonder if I'll ever see her again. If she'll come back before it's too late. If she'll succeed in convincing her father – or if she will change her mind when it's already too late.

I take a step through the doorway, but Lez blocks my way, staring at me with a daunting gaze.

"Such a lovely, lovely story of yours," he sneers. "Family rivalries, magic flutes, claiming to be Hamelin's saint. What kind of girl wouldn't fall for this fantastic fairy tale? But it just leaves one riddle to be answered: WHERE ARE THE CHILDREN?"

"You don't -"

"I do understand. I'm just asking the thousand-guilder question that Hamelin has wondered ever since you last set foot in this town and broke the hearts of every family. Now, tell me: Where do I find this dynasty of yours to bring back what we're searching for?"

"You can't -"

"I CAN!" he roars, his shaky voice cracking. "Leave the girl alone and tell me where it is. I will bring them back myself!"

He frowns and takes out one of my flutes from his pouch. He holds it in his two hands and feigns breaking it in half if I don't give him the response he wants.

"What's going on here?" Captain Hook interrupts, swinging his hooked hand. "We don't need any playground fights in this prison, now, do we?"

To my advantage, Lez is clearly terrified of the prison keeper. He puts away the flute, preparing to leave.

"Go on now, Mr. Hoffner. Time for the Pied Piper's last bath before the big event tomorrow."

Oh, so now they give me a bath. Conveniently after my "date" with Snowphia!

If being imprisoned here wasn't so bothersome, I'd be laughing about this whole ordeal.

***

"You're home early," Mr. Blumenthal said, as Snowphia dragged herself through the corridor to the kitchen.

"Yeah," she mumbled, unfastening her cloak, and sliding off her headscarf. Her eyes were still glossy from having cried on her way home.

"Everything ok?"

"I didn't have much to do today, so they let me off early." Snowphia took out a cluster of carrots and a head of cabbage, proceeding to chop them on the breadboard.

Mr. Blumenthal was quite sure there was more to the story that she was hiding.

"How's Mama?" Snowphia asked.

"As usual. She's sleeping."

"You're home early yourself, Papa."

"We had to receive Albert, the executioner from England today."

Snowphia held her breath at the thought. She stumbled towards the chair, feeling faint. Her father caught her just in time.

"What did he do to you?" Mr. Blumenthal exclaimed resentfully. "We'll have him executed tonight if he laid a hand on you!"

Snowphia shook her head and tried to pull herself back together.

"It's nothing like that," she murmured. "I promise you."

Just then Mr. Blumenthal noticed the glisten of the white pearl necklace glinting on her pale, freckled skin.

"Where on earth did you get those?"

Snowphia took a deep breath and stood up straight, smoothing out her skirt as if nothing had happened.

"From the Pied Piper, Papa."

"What?"

"He's asked me to marry him."

"WHAT?"

"We'll have to marry tonight because he's going to die tomorrow."

"Are you crazy, my daughter?" Mr. Blumenthal slumped into the wooden chair. "You cannot marry a man on death row."

"Why not?"

"Because-"

"Because you'll never let me marry," Snowphia cut him off.

"I never said that, did I?"

"You said it to the Pied Piper himself."

Mr. Blumenthal scratched his head. "Snowphia, you must understand, after Maddie, we're just afraid -"

"Maddie is alive."

"That I doubt, my daughter."

"They all are alive," Snowphia said more firmly. "You'll see. They're coming back soon."

"Don't consume yourself with such hopeful illusions -"

"He told me. You'll see."

Mr. Blumenthal sighed.

"We're going to marry tonight, Father."

"And what will you get out of all of this?" Mr. Blumenthal demanded. "A dead man as your husband? That is no way to live. At the very least, find a man who has more than a day ahead of him."

"We will be rich, Father. He's offering you a bride price of 100,000 gold coins, and even more in precious stones if that doesn't convince you enough. We can repair our house for the cold winters. We can eat well. We can afford a nurse for Mama. We can wear the finest textiles and at last, have enough money for more than modest gifts for Christmas."

"What makes you think this man is really as wealthy as he claims to be?" Mr. Blumenthal challenged.

Snowphia slipped out of the kitchen and went directly to the room where the Pied Piper had stayed the other night. There, Chuka was playing with Snowphia's brush and an old doll.

"Hey, you!" she joked, pulling them out of his tiny, hairy hands. "What are you doing with those?"

"I got bored while you were gone."

Snowphia's eyes widened. Had he just talked? Maybe she was imagining things…

Or maybe the Pied Piper was right about having talking animals as his pets.

"Looking for this?" Chuka asked with a grin, pulling out a handful of shiny rubies from the pouch he'd carried all the way from Guernsey.

"Yes!"

Chuka poured them into her palm.

"Father! Come here!" Snowphia called.

"Who in heaven's name are you talking to in there -?"

"Hello," Chuka greeted with a simper.

"We all must be losing our minds," Mr. Blumenthal gasped to himself, clutching his chest as though his heart might jump right out.

"Look, Father." Snowphia opened her palm to reveal the crimson gems twinkling next to the candlelight. "He has many more of these. He told me where to find them."

Mr. Blumenthal took them into his hands and studied them up close. If they weren't rubies, he didn't know what they could be.

It then dawned on him. It is said that when a man faces death, he reflects on his life and seeks redemption for all of his wrongdoings. He who is about to leave this world does whatever is in his power to make sure all debts are paid before he crosses to the other side. Mr. Blumenthal remembered the guilt in the Pied Piper's eyes when they spoke of Maddie and what losing her had done to the family. What harm could a simple marriage do if the Piper would no longer exist tomorrow?

"What do you think?" Snowphia asked, a hint of hope in her countenance.

"I think I like this Dead Man's Proposal," he replied. "We have a ceremony to arrange."

***

The smell of musk and rose leaves when they bring me to a dim room illuminated solely by a candelabra. It's the same room where Snowphia treated my wounds. On the table is a small feast of roasted meat, potatoes, and pickled cabbage.

"Dinner for one?" I comment in awe.

"It's your last meal," the Gustavo replies, nearly throwing me to the chair. How cordial of him.

"So, I'm clean-shaven and I'm being treated to a candlelight supper. All that's missing is a lady to impress with all of it," I say frankly.

"Eat up," the Gustavo instructs.

"I'm vegan," I protest.

"What does that mean? Well then, we'll throw the roast to Charlie."

Having second thoughts, I shake no with my hand. I'm going to need to recuperate my energy before I flee this place. I pick up the juicy, rare meat with my hands and devour it piece by piece. I've barely eaten in days, and you could tell.

Spooning up my pickled cabbage, I begin thinking about Snowphia again, wondering what has happened with her father. Hours have passed, and I'm increasingly losing my hopes of her returning. I eye Captain Hook pacing back and forth in the hallway. My only consolation is that perhaps any minute, he'll bring me a nun who can excuse me out of the jail and accompany me to the church where Snowphia will be waiting.

I lose sight of the Captain. He's no longer in the corridor.

"No visits allowed this late!" His loud voice echoes down the hallway.

Then another voice enters the conversation. A woman's voice. It's Snowphia.

I strain to listen to what they're saying.

"Take twenty gold coins," Mr. Blumenthal's voice says. "It's from the Piper himself."

There's a pause, and then some words I can't make out.

"Marry him?" I finally hear the Captain shout. "Are you mad? He's a criminal and his head will be in a basket by dusk tomorrow!"

"It's not your business," Mr. Blumenthal replies. "These are my wishes, and this is my daughter."

"Well, then," the Captain replies, jingling the coins in his pocket. "I can't deny a father's wishes for his daughter, now can I?"

A chorus of footsteps reverberates down the stone corridor. A guffaw sounds from the dungeon.

"The Pied Piper's getting married!" Charlie's voice howls. "She's a whore, I tell you! A whore! Only a whore would marry a prisoner!"

I am sure that Mr. Blumenthal is huffing at the insulting words, because I sure as hell am.

When I look up from the potato, I see her blue eyes watching me from the doorway. I quickly scrub my lips with my tunic sleeve, hoping I haven't made a mess of myself from the haphazard meal.

I stand up and Snowphia and I both smirk at each other. Without words, we know what we mean to say.

"I'm ready," she murmurs.

***

We arrive at St. Nicolai church on the unicorn horse. Snowphia sits behind me with her arms wrapped snugly around my chest. Mr. Blumenthal is beside us on a horse that he's rented for the occasion. Surprisingly, he doesn't look twice at our overt affection. I'm not sure if it's because his mind is preoccupied with the bride price, or if he feels sorry for me knowing that I'm scheduled to die tomorrow.

We march down the aisle between the pews, candles illuminating the white pillars and gold-trimmed archways. At the altar, the priest is preparing for the Christmas Eve midnight mass.

"Father Albrecht," Mr. Blumenthal addresses. "I hate to bother you at this hour, but as you can imagine, this is an urgent matter."

The priest's eyes turn to me, looking me up and down.

"Is that… the Pied Piper?" he stammers in disbelief.

"That I am," I agree. "Well, not so 'pied' anymore in these prison clothes, I have to admit."

"You've come for the last confession; I reckon?"

"Not exactly," Mr. Blumenthal clarifies. "I've come to ask your service in the matter of… marrying my daughter."

The priest's mouth falls open. "What?"

"Our unfortunate friend, the Pied Piper, has proposed to my daughter as his one final wish before his execution, and she has accepted."

Mr. Blumenthal's enthusiasm shocks me, but by the priest's frown, I can see he is far less keen on our engagement.

"I will not marry a man who has not yet lifted the burden of sin from his soul," Father Albrecht asserts.

"I believe I can remedy that," Mr. Blumenthal assures. He takes out a sack of gold coins that I'd left behind in the family's house. "I am willing to pay indulgences on behalf of the Pied Piper. And as you know, my daughter has been devout to the church for all her life, and the Lord would undoubtedly advocate for her happiness on such a crucial occasion."

Father Albrecht hesitates, assessing each of us.

Mr. Blumenthal, an aspiring politician, seems to enjoy this exercise in rhetoric. "Don't you think, Father, that the sacredness of love alone would not perhaps pardon a man's sins?"

He forces the sack of the coins into Father Albrecht's hands.

"I do think the kind Lord would approve."

It seems that the priest realizes it will take more effort to disagree and remove us from the premises than to go along with the union.

"Just a short ceremony," Mr. Blumenthal insists. "No need for vows or kisses. Let's just get this over with."

The priest clears his throat. "Pied Piper and Snowphia Blumenthal, have you come here to enter into marriage without coercion, freely, and wholeheartedly?"

Snowphia and I glance at each other.

"Yes."

"Yes."

"Are you prepared, as you follow the path of marriage, to love and honour each other for as long as you both shall live?"

"It's less than a day!" Mr. Blumenthal exclaims. "Now get on with it. I'd like to discuss the bride price with you, Mr. Piper, once we're finished."

Father Albrecht glares at him for the interruption. He skims down the list of vows he has before him, skipping to the important part.

"Pied Piper, do you take Snowphia Blumenthal to be your lawful wife, to have and to hold, from this day forward, for better, for worse, for richer, for poorer, in sickness and in health, until death do you part?"

My heart thumps. It's only in this moment that I reflect on where I'm standing, and who is standing before me. Just a week ago, I was dreaming of the mysterious maiden of Hamelin that my ravens told me was the perfect woman for me. And here I am, attesting my devotion to her. I am marrying her. The fact finally sinks in.

Now, let's hope I live to see her tomorrow.

"I do."

"Snowphia Blumenthal, do you take the Pied Piper to be your lawful husband, to have and to hold, from this day forward, for better, for worse, for richer, for poorer, in sickness and in health, until death do you part?"

"I do," she murmurs.

"I now pronounce you husband and wife."

I take Snowphia into my arms and kiss her forehead. "Thank you for letting me love," I whisper in her ear. "I look forward to your love."

"So do I," she whispers back.

I'm overjoyed to hear these mere three words.

"I need to explain the rest of the plan to you," I whisper to her, still embracing her to hide from the priest and Mr. Blumenthal what I'm saying. "On the way back to the prison."

***

I pretend to be drifting into sleep, but the escape plan is running through my head on repeat. As to be expected, Crooks and Charlie are obnoxiously snoring on either side of me, so even if I want to sleep, it doesn't seem likely that I'll be able to.

Planning an escape sounds more fun than what it is. I've come to the realization that without magic, I'm not quite as clever as I'd like to think.

I hear the door unlatch and a pool of candlelight extends across the floor.

"Wakey, wakey," the Gustavo commands, unlocking my shackles.

"What on earth…?" I grumble irritably.

"There's a midnight visitor for you."

I panic, worried that I'm going to receive news of something having gone amiss. Maybe Snowphia's been found out? Even worse, perhaps someone has hurt her?

The Gustavo has one mighty grip for a man who's as small as he, tugging my wrists as I trudge behind him down the corridor. He brings me to the infamous room that has hosted so many events during my time here.

He sits me down, and one of the guards' escorts in a towering man with dishevelled blond hair and piercing blue eyes that make him looked like he alone has pillaged a few villages in his lifetime.

"Meet Albert, your executioner," the Gustavo introduces with a sadistic wink. "Commissioned from London."

Albert sits in front of me, glaring at me with a stony expression.

I don't even wince. Maybe it's because I've already had my head chopped off, in my imagination, that is. Or maybe it's because I'm so relieved that it's not bad news for Snowphia that he doesn't even scare me.

"Pleased to meet you," he rasps, extending his massive hand. I accept, regretting it as I feel my fingers being crushed in his powerful grip.

"Likewise," I mumble.

"Are you ready for your big day?"

I tilt my head. "More ready than most men, you could say."

He raises his eyebrows at the unexpected nonchalance in my tone. The giant leans forward, fixating my eyes with his two savage orbs.

"Never have I looked into the eyes of a man about to die who shows no fear of what is about to come," he mutters, in an eerie calm that makes it seem like he's about to jump up and choke me.

"That is because you've already killed me before," I reason. "In my nightmares."

The man chuckles. "I take that as a compliment."

***

The Mayor yawned, then sneezed, taking out his handkerchief to blow his nose. He shoved the drenched cloth back into his pocket.

"Come on, already," he moaned to himself, shivering outside the prison as he waited for Albert to finish up his business. The giant dipped through the low archway, the Captain escorting him from behind.

"There you are," the Mayor greeted. "All set and settled with the Piper?"

"I tell you, gentleman," Albert attested. "I've executed 200 men - strong men, even knights put to death for treason - but never in my life has one looked me straight in the eye without fear. Either he is confident he will escape, or he has a heart of stone."

"Escape!" Not believing his ears, Captain Hook clumsily swung his hook towards the Mayor, who jumped in place. "I've never had a prisoner escape, nor will it ever happen."

Unconvinced, Albert flashed a forced smile which looked more like he was gritting his teeth.

***

The church bells chimed eight times, and Snowphia knew she had no time to lose. The Pied Piper's execution was scheduled for noon that day.

Light, fluffy snowflakes fluttered through the air in the chill morning, as she sped down the street, trying not to slip on the icy cobblestones. She reached St. Nicolai church, where she'd been wed the previous night. Just as planned, Snowphia found the nuns filtering out of the nearby convent with hymnals and bibles to distribute to the town.

"He refused to confess," she heard the last nun say to the sister next to her. "Refused! Can you imagine? And his execution is today!"

Luckily, given how absorbed the woman was in gossiping – obviously about her now-husband – Snowphia managed to catch the door before it latched shut. She scurried down the arched corridor, turning the corner, looking through each opened door. Finally, she reached a room with a big wardrobe standing on the farthest wall.

"Aha!"

Snowphia tugged open the door and found stack upon stack of grey nuns' habits. She retrieved one gown, a white wimple, a black veil, and a scapular that was hanging from the hook on the inside door.

After changing into her new outfit, she sought the library. Just as she'd thought, she found an apothecary table with stacks of bibles in each drawer.

Snowphia the Nun rolled the table through the snow, which crunched with every step until she reached the town square.

Just then, a little girl passed her in tears, bawling about how Santa hadn't left her anything to wake up to that morning.

"Dry your tears, child," Snowphia cooed, pulling out a brand-new doll from the sack she was carrying. It was one of the toys the Pied Piper had picked up in London.

The little girl's eyes lit up. She took the stuffed toy, cuddling it in her arms.

"Why, thank you!" the mother exclaimed. "That wasn't something I expected to happen in this godforsaken town."

"The church is feeling very generous today," Snowphia reasoned. "Our indulgences are more than anticipated, and well, we have the fortune of celebrating that justice will be served for the child thief."

"Indeed," the woman replied, nodding respectfully, and taking her daughter's hand before waving goodbye to the generous nun.

Snowphia heaved a sigh of relief and got on her way. She did her best to avoid attention from the nuns who were gifting bibles to passers-by. No one would notice what was peeking underneath her robes.

"Who is that?" one of them asked, as they watched the mysterious nun rolling an apothecary table with a huge canvas sack planted on top of it. Their eyes followed Snowphia as she disappeared from the town square.

She turned around a corner, with their secret weapon hidden inside her tightly closed robes. She smiled a beatific smile and waved at the children playing around the streets.

***

Even in the dungeon, the knocking at the prison door resonates like thunder. It jolts me awake. For a moment I forget where I am or how I got here. When it comes back to me that it's the day of my execution, I wonder how I managed to sleep at all last night.

I overhear the conversation at the door.

"I'm here to lead the prayer before the Pied Piper's execution," Snowphia's voice says.

Bravo! She's gotten this far in the plan. It's no simple task, but I had faith a clever woman like her could pull it off.

"Well, I wasn't informed of this," Captain Hook argues.

"I've been sent with some gifts too," she adds, apparently handing him something. "The church wishes you a Merry Christmas and a happy retirement."

Before I know it, Snowphia's led into our dungeon by the Gustavo. Behind them is Captain Hook, holding a green, heart-shaped gourd. He's turning it, trying to figure out what it is.

"That's a watermelon, you fool," Charlie shouts.

"Is it?" Captain Hook asks, looking at Snowphia.

"It's moulded fruit," she clarifies. "I take it you've never seen it before?"

Captain Hook shrugs his shoulders. It's the first time I've seen him behave like a little boy. Snowphia opens the drawers of the apothecary table and takes out enough bibles to pass around.

"I'm afraid you're going to have to unshackle them, so they can open the books with their own hands. Now that the snowstorm has ceased, perhaps we could hold the session in the courtyard, so we are better in touch with the heavens."

The Gustavo turns towards Captain Hook, who is still studying the melon.

"What was that?" The Captain finally looks up to find all eyes staring at him.

"So?" the Gustavo asks.

"Oh, yes, yes, whatever Sister what's-her-name sees fit," he grumbles.

"Sister Anne," says Snowphia primly, in a perfect imitation of the prim-and-proper icy tone of the nuns of the town.

I turn to Crooks in disbelief. Did Captain Hook really agree to let us out of the dungeon? The Captain proceeds to pace back and forth as usual, but this time, throwing the heart-shaped watermelon in the air like a ball and catching it.

"Are you sure this is a watermelon?" he asks Snowphia.

But before he gets an answer, the prisoners are already lined up behind Snowphia and the Gustavo to file out into the courtyard.

"W-wait!" he shouts behind them. "What's going on?"

Snowphia conveniently leaves the apothecary table behind. I hear Captain Hook's footsteps trail down the corridor. That gives me just enough time to squeeze myself into the hollow table.

Snowphia coughs exaggeratedly and I look down chastened.

"What are we going to do?" she mouths.

"Did you find the coins?" I mouth back.

She nods.

"Did you find all my things?" I ask low, coming closer to her to kneel in a position of obedient prayer.

She furrows her brow.

"What do you mean?" she asks.

I trace the pattern of an instrument with my hands and, when she doesn't realize what I'm talking about, I mimic the sound of the flute.

Her eyes open wide.

"Here," she mouths, pointing at the interior of her robes.

I blush slightly and she turns bright red.

"It's on an internal pocket," she says lowly.

"What are we going to do?"

"Follow my lead," he says slowly.

"I like it that you're going through this plan without so much fear. I'm dying here," her lips tremble as she hands me the flute.

"I like it that you have so much faith in me, wife," I say, and she gives me a small smile.

"Not for long if you don't do anything about it," she says.

"It's time for us to be the best actors we can be. Are you ready?"

She nods and gives me a side-eyed smile.

"Try not to get us killed, sir. I quite like the idea of you being my husband," she says shakily.

Oh, how I love this woman.

***

The guards have sequestered us to the outside, complying with a nun's wish to publicly help me go through penitence and worship of the Lord.

"These aren't good men, but they fear the Lord just like you do now, sir," she says coldly.

I look at her feigning indifference and malice.

"I've come to help your soul through the process of leaving this world unperturbed. It is part of my duty to tend to the wounds in your soul and soothe you through your final moments. Would you go through this faithfully and accordingly with our Lord's plan?"

"Then, my dear nun, if you're going to save my soul, it will have to be now," I say looking at her with distaste.

She stares at me, with her innocent and bottomless ocean eyes, and without even blinking, she responds. "Yes."

"I wish to convert to the proper path our Lord has shaped for us sinners," I say without any trace of warmth lingering in my voice. It shakes with false regret to make sure it makes people notice my fear, and the struggle I'm having.

I look around- only a few people are looking at us and, even the guards are relaxed, speaking. I know they're relaxed because they're stronger than me, and as I'm unarmed, I don't pose any threat for them.

She notices it too and gives me a half-smile that makes my heart race wildly.

"If only so you can walk away the filth of this cell from your skin and lungs before you're executed?" she asks giving me a small wink before going back to her acting.

I chuckle. "If you can coax enough patience from my guard to do so, I could use a good walk."

I could use running away from here, but I'm not telling her this in front of this people. Nevertheless, she has to bite her lip to avoid laughing. She cocks her head, her gaze unwavering. Then, she stands and walks to the door.

"Thank you," she says when the guard escorts us outside of the room. "And please, find another guard. We're taking the prisoner to the river for his baptism."

"Alright, don't think I trust your intentions, if you say anything, you're going to win the beating of a lifetime and my whip will leave your body marked. Not that it'd matter anymore, as you'll die before anyone gets to see that," he says mockingly, and I walk behind him and Snowphia.

The fake nun leads us to the streets, droning prayers. I do my best keeping my head bowed in a posture of penitence, my dirty hair hiding my equally dirty face, wondering if they know there's something off and what we're planning. She's no fool. Her part of the devout and innocent pious nun has been played to perfection, yes, but not a fool. And of my three companions, she's the one who worries me the most. Snowphia leads me -the condemned man- through the streets, intoning some prayers all the way. As she prays, I wonder how, exactly, she's learned these prayers. Surely, she has seen many penitent men in the years she's spent at the prison, ministering to men condemned to die and cleansing their bodies. Perhaps, she's heard confessions from them too and if there's one thing she knows, it's that The Pied Piper is worth it.

As for me, as I walk through the streets, escorted like the very worst of the criminals, I think she's meant to convert any man to the most unlike paths or any faith, whichever she professes currently or to any of the faiths currently in the world.

Nevertheless, the gleam in her eyes is still too cunning, too teasing, even after two sleepless nights and knowing her –recently known- husband's death which is only a few moments away.

I am not a man afraid to die. That is because I am a man that isn't going to die today or anytime soon! I stumble a little at the thought and the two guards escorting me snicker.

"You're not as agile anymore, not like you were when you ran away from the men that sought justice for you."

"And this nun won't be able to do anything for you. You're so rotten that the depths of hell must be buzzing with gleefulness at knowing where you are headed."

I have to refrain from slapping them with my magic right then and there. But they mustn't know that my hands aren't tied yet.

No, let them gloat all they want.

Not even her nun's robes could shield the ire radiating from her at the sound of their mockery. Her anger flares and fades just as quickly.

"Are you all right, nun?" I murmur, seeking her eyes briefly to let her know that it's almost over, and she spares me a glance and a quick nod.

I flash her a grin. "Good. I'd hate to see you injure yourself before you've saved me," I say lowly.

"As would I, my dear," she says in a very low voice.

One of the guards gives me a hard shove and this time, it's my feet that slips. I cry out with pain as I fall to my knees on the sharp rocks, the noise of the chains and shackles loud in the quiet streets.

Snowphia looks at me worried.

"Help us!" she says sharply, and hurries to help me to my feet.

"Thank you, sister," I say.

"Are you going to let his pretty face distract you?" calls the second guard, and Snowphia hastily steps away.

She turns to the speaker and gives him a steady stare. "I'll pray for your soul as well, Mr. We're not as good as we often believe we are. It'd do you well to search in your heart before casting the first stone against a sinner. Perhaps, you should ask yourself what kind of life you're leading" she says and continues leading the way to the river.

***

We finally make it to a new street where we have a bigger audience, having been slowed down by my scraped and bruised knees. It stings a little, but it's nothing I haven't felt before. Like the scrapped knee of a child, these scars will heal soon.

Snowphia orders the guards to unshackle me before leading me into the quiet crowd. People look thin and dishevelled just like the first time after the missing children incident.

"I am not a good actress," she reminds me, as she grabs my arm, doing her best imitation of a stern nun, but failing miserably.

"I've only done this once and my audience wasn't quite as big as this one."

I nod along.

"I have a last request," I say slowly.

"What is that, sir?" she asks me.

"I know what I have to do and I hope you'll be able to help me through it," I reply, "but as long as you remind me the words that I have to say, that should be enough."

"It's not the words, Mr. Pied Piper," Snowphia says, "it's what you truly believe in your heart."

I believe you look like my one true saviour under the light of day, I think. But I only say, "Yes, you're right." I lower my voice. "I hadn't expected you to always be right."

Her eyes widen, and I think they're the most beautiful eyes I've ever seen.

"I hadn't expected you to be this way either," she replies, her voice too quiet for the guards to hear. "You're gentler than what you've been given credit of."

She smiles, and under the bright lights, I can see she's flushing furiously. She looks away, then begins the prayers and a small look passes between us before she does it, her fingertips resting lightly on my forehead, then dropping to my chest, following the sign of the cross.

If I wasn't going through an elaborate list of things to do, I'd be terrified of being used for mass prayer. She finishes the prayer, and then comes the moment of truth.

This is where everything turns decisive. I look at her from the corner of my eye and feel magic coursing through me. Our eyes meet once again under the broad daylight and I know that I should lower myself and show my repentant posture in front of these people. If she lowers me, I'll be able to reach for something—

She gives me a hard push on the shoulders and I relax, allowing myself to fall on my knees into the water—and then I'm beneath the surface of the barrier and I'm kicking and gliding away as quickly as I can, as if I am going through water.

I break the invisible surface for breath, and hear the guards shouting behind me, Snowphia's excited voice, and then I go under again as the crack of a gunshot rings in my ears. The guards escort Snowphia, looking ready to bring her to immediate justice, but she isn't letting them win.

In short order, a number of things happen; I get myself outside the invisible camp surrounding me and grab Snowphia by the arm, whisking her away as the executioner is brought from his quarters, along with the Mayor and Captain Hook. It's clear we've destroyed their plans to have the Pied Piper under their clutches and displaying my head on the walls.

A scream, coming from Captain Hook is heard as Snowphia and I contemplate one another inside our own secluded space.

"I'm sorry," I say. "I almost thought they would get to you before me. And they did in a way! You must be so angry with me. I know you don't care for me the same way I do, but it's my duty as your husband to provide shelter and comfort for you-"

"Silence, Your Highness. Somehow, I don't think this is the worst thing that's going to happen. And you should let me decide how I feel about my dear husband," she adds passionately before grabbing my hand firmly.

The Judge is frantic too. He and the Mayor immediately send out search parties, then turns his attention to her. His eyes are coldly triumphant.

"I WANT HIM TO BE WHIPPED, AND WE MUST BEHEAD HIM ONCE AND FOR ALL. He'll have one-hundred lashes. Then, take the girl here."

"She'll have her punishment. One she deserves this time. We can't be too lenient here; she must learn what happens to the traitors and Pipers!"

The silent streets revolt.

"What happened?" asks a woman in a hushed tone.

"Was that magic?"

"He's evil and took that poor nun with him! Poor woman will endure hell on Earth, I don't envy her destiny," says another woman.

"It's indeed unfortunate," adds a man.

***

Back where Snowphia left the children, they were gleefully unaware of the ruckus. In that street, the children were playing merrily with the gifts brought by her. The Piper dropped her there before disappearing to pick up his unicorns and the other pets, and she stood there and watched the girls play.

"Look at my new doll!" the little girl shrieked, waving it in front of her neighbour, a boy around the same age.

"I got a puppet!" he exclaimed, tilting the wooden handle back and forth to make the marionette move. She suddenly noticed she wasn't the only adult observing the heart-warming scene.

It was Lez.

***

"She said the church was 'feeling good,'..." Lez heard one of the mothers explain to the other, eavesdropping as he passed the peasant children bragging about their new gifts. "The church is unusually generous this year."

"Humph," he grunted to himself. Lez knew there was something fishy about this equation. The church was the last institution to give gifts during the holiday season. He was sure it was the Pied Piper's presents that the children had received – but who had gotten a hold of them and how?

An even stranger spectacle that caught his sight was a nun ploughing through the middle of the town square with a wheeled table. Perhaps he could cook up a juicy news story about all these oddities, he reasoned to himself.

"Sister, might I help you with that?" he feigned politeness.

"No, thank you," Snowphia replied, picking up speed to pass him up.

Lez caught up with her again.

"You must be handing out gifts for the church, as I've heard?"

"Oh no," she insisted, trying to move even faster, but the thick snow worked against her. In her frenzy, her wimple began to slide down her head. "It must have been one of my sisters."

The pearl necklace caught Lez's attention. He remembered them. From where, though? Then, her vivid eyes lit a memory on his mind.

Snowphia, the prison nurse.

He had to get to the bottom of this.

"Lovely necklace you have there. I thought nuns didn't wear jewellery."

Snowphia was sure Lez wasn't just flirting.

"Sorry, kind sir. No time for small talk. I'm scheduled to be at the convent."

Lez refused to fall behind her.

"I heard the church was gifting bibles to the townspeople. Might I have one?"

"Oh my, forgive me, but we've run out of them."

"Are you sure?" he demanded. "Open the drawers and show me!"

Snowphia was terrified. Just when everything up until then had gone exactly as planned, she couldn't let them be caught by some stupid, obnoxious slanderer.

Lez violently grabbed Snowphia's arm, forcing her to slow her pace. By then, passers-by were already staring at the commotion.

"What are you doing?" she shrieked.

"Leave her alone! She's a woman of God!" a man shouted, angrily pointing his walking stick at Lez.

"She's a phony!" he shouted back, yanking out the drawers one by one and letting them drop to the snow.

Snowphia's jaw dropped, seeing the inside of the table was empty.

"I'm merely here to give a dying man all the succour he needs in the name of the Lord."

"But I'm guessing that if you don't like the presence of the church here, you won't like my sisters doing their routine here either. They clean, feed, and listen to the most deranged criminals and this Piper is no exception," she says spitting out the word 'Piper'.

What they didn't know was that she handed the man his escape weapon: another one of his instruments.

She touched it without thinking and then he appeared around the corner. "Hop in! NOW!" he exclaimed as he worked his magic to make Lez fall asleep while she ran to take his side on top of Storm.

She'd never been more grateful for a musical instrument.

CHAPTER 12

KOPPELBERG HILL

The unicorn horse slowly trekked up Koppelberg Hill. Chuka's fuzzy arms were wrapped around Snowphia's shoulders like a knapsack, trying to keep warm against the frigid air of wonderland. The trees glittered silver under the hazy morning sky.

"Do we go left or right from here?" Snowphia asked.

"Take a right up to the plateau here," Chuka advised. "Let's hope a hungry beaver hasn't dug up the gems and confused them for Christmas candy."

The unicorn horse took a few more steps, and Snowphia pulled the reins to halt him. She swung her leg over and jumped to the snowy ground. When she let Chuka down, he went directly to the burrow and began digging out the snow with his dexterous hands. Beneath it, emerged a cluster of royal blue velvet drawstring bags. He pulled them out, dusting off the snowflakes. She was oddly reminded of the worms for Spinky. She made a mental note to let her Prince know about it. The poor thing must be hungry.

"This one is for Mr. Blumenthal," Chuka instructed, handing one of them to her. "The Piper left it here just for the occasion."

He opened his own leather pouch and dropped the smaller of the velvet bags into it. "And this one is to get us back to Guernsey."

Snowphia pensively remained kneeling in the snow. "Does he always disappear just like that?"

"He's a nimble one," Chuka told her. "Don't forget he's not from our world."

"What if he doesn't come back?" Snowphia sulked.

"Oh, he will."

"Why wouldn't I?" a deep voice murmured from behind them.

A tall figure emerged from the shadows of the trees. It was the Pied Piper. He extended his arm to help up Snowphia, and then propped Chuka on his shoulders.

"A vow is a vow," he said to her. "I never go back on a vow."

The two leaned in for a warm embrace.

***

I sit on a colossal rock at the peak of the hill, the chilly wind combing through the strands of my dark hair. Chuka has gone with Snowphia, and giving his knack for directions, I predict they'll return in no time, so we can be on our way to Guernsey.

A figure that appears to be limping emerges from between the trees. He has a walking stick, a triangle cap, and a long blue cape. He approaches me, close enough that I can catch a glimpse of his face.

"There you are," Lez's whiny voice declares. "I thought I'd seen the prison nurse hike up this hill on a strange creature."

I know him; he's the young man that has been writing about how I poisoned the river to kill all the fishes and leave Hamelin without food. How I made kids run straight to their death. And the one I hate the most: that it was all a ruse, a plot from the neighbouring nations to make sure Hamelin does whatever they want to do.

I look at Lez's expectant face, feeling remorse, pain and shudders go up my spine as we stare at each other. A shadow seems to hide inside those eyes. I must have wronged this man and he's here for vengeance.

"You didn't realize who I was when you came here," says Lez slowly. His voice shakes slightly as he speaks.

"But I've always known who you are, Pied Piper. At first, you were a stranger that came in to fulfil your word."

He takes a deep breath.

"Now, you're here to make up for what you did at first. To you, these children matter and that's how you'd like to be remembered: as someone that cared about the children. Not as a child killer."

"I was one of those children, I'm the child you left behind. I followed you, the melody was so beautiful, and I couldn't stop dancing, even if I commanded my body not to do so at first. Then, I gave in, and the promises of a better life, a peaceful life with plenty of music, magic and good food would be at the ready for any child that was good! I allowed myself to dream big and followed your path, but my legs weren't good even then, and that let me fall behind, stranded. I went back and was frustrated to be the only one left behind, but I was sure that your promise wasn't a farce. Although, now I know it was an unfortunate accident, I was sad and angered at being separated from the other children. But I've never thought that they were dead," he makes a pause, balancing the weight of a foot with his cane.

"This is why I want to join you; I won't stay behind this time. It's been my life's worth to know where they are!" he says, eyes shining, and jaw firmly set.

He's a courageous, selfless young man, I'll give him that, which is how I find myself doubting my plans; would bringing him along be a good decision? Or would it be solely based on his need to be a do-gooder? He hasn't explained why he's endorsed such horrible lies about me. I don't have any solid reason to believe his word.

His first words move me and fill me with remorse. I hadn't turned around once when I'd played my flute, so hastily trying to bring the children to safety. Never would I have imagined the poor boy had been left behind. Just then, I spot the unicorn horse in the distance, making its way up the hill. Thankfully, Snowphia and Chuka have made it back quicker than expected.

"We're ready," Snowphia exhales with an accomplished smile. "All went as planned. Nobody gave me trouble in the town. The townspeople seem a bit restless today though."

She is looking at Chuka as she speaks, but then she turns and sees Lez and lets out a scream.

I give her a calming look.

"Calm down, dear. Snowphia, he's here to tell me -us- something of utmost importance."

Lez looks at us both before speaking.

"I'm sorry that I behaved the way I did. I don't want any of you to believe that I am happily spreading lies out of my own free will."

I raise an eyebrow at that. I don't see where he's heading with all this.

"I made people believe so many lies to appease the ire of the Mayor. That vile man would have done something awful to me if I hadn't done what he wanted. You see, I needed to work to live and he offered things to me – things that I knew he wouldn't do, mind you- but he offered them, nevertheless. So, here I am, willing to let you know that what I did was wrong and that, maybe doing it wasn't only to appease the Mayor. That I had another motivation in mind when I agreed to publish those lies."

Perhaps believing his story is foolish, but there's nothing much he can do here other than what I want. And now Snowphia is listening to his tale patiently, but regarding him with a serious expression that I've seen before. She's most likely wondering if what he's saying is true. I don't know if I can trust him, but I do believe it's true. He seems sincere, nicer than the pig of the Mayor of Hamelin and his eyes are shining as he speaks.

Although, I could be wrong. So, my flute is nearby if he attempts anything funny.

"I made those stories and published them so that the Mayor would stop harassing me, but also to keep your mind in this town and why you were needed here."

My mouth drops slightly.

It can't be!

"But why didn't you tell me about it? Surely, you must have wanted to confront me, like everybody in here does. I almost went insane with grief and guilt once I realized the children were missing."

"That's something I care about too," he recognizes, nodding. "That's why I'm here. To apologize for the pain caused through my preposterous lies, and to ask you to let me go with you; I'm sure you're going to save those children wherever you go, and I want to be part of it."

"You could be part of it. We're just a bit perplexed because there's so many things that have happened to us and the people of Hamelin."

I don't know if I should take his word for it, but I'm going to accept it for now.

"What about all those things you wrote about me with that sharp pen of yours? You claim it was something you were made to do, but I've read them, and I know the Mayor."

"I realize my behaviour was reckless, but I know the path ahead of us is going to be fruitful and make us learn where these children are."

"Alright, you may come, but know that I don't do any of those things your paper accused me of doing and if I ever find you embellishing the truth, I'll be the one passing judgement."

And with that, I end the conversation and let Lez join us in our grand escape. After all, it's only a matter of time until we reach the missing children and bring them home.

The End

www.ingramcontent.com/pod-product-compliance
Lightning Source LLC
Chambersburg PA
CBHW021223250626
47155CB00008B/2911